TO THE STARS

Also by

L. RON HUBBARD

* Dekalogy—a group of ten volumes

L. RON HUBBARD

TO THE STARS

GALAXY PRESS

PUBLISHER OF THE FICTION WORKS OF L. RON HUBBARD

TO THE STARS

Produced by Galaxy Press, L.L.C.
7051 Hollywood Boulevard, Suite 200
Hollywood, CA 90028

Cover & Book design: Mike Manoogian
Printed in the United States of America
2 3 4 5 6 7 8 9 10

ISBN: 1-59212-175-6

Library of Congress Control Number: 2004106845

INTRODUCTION

In the December 1949 issue of *Astounding Science Fiction*, editor John W. Campbell, Jr., announced that the magazine would publish "a new, remarkably powerful novel" by L. Ron Hubbard, starting in February of the following year. Campbell promoted it again in January 1950, writing, "It's a two-parter, and a beautiful development of the theme based on the time-rate differential of ships traveling near the speed of light."

The reaction of readers was an unmistakable indication that the novel *To the Stars* more than lived up to Campbell's praise and endorsement. Each month *Astounding* would hold a readers' poll, a tabulation of the popularity of stories in the previous issues, based upon cards and letters from fans. And by the June 1950 issue, Campbell was announcing:

> *To the Stars* took top place in the March issue; judging from the character of the letters, it deserved it. And the sequence of stories seems to follow neatly, and exactly, the degree of thought required to appreciate the tale. The plot of *To the Stars* called forth a number of technical letters and evidently stirred a lot of thinking.

The story not only stimulated technical speculation but also inspired a considerable amount of reader enthusiasm, such as this from William N. Austin of The Wolf Den Book Shop in Seattle, Washington. After criticizing another story, Austin went on to say:

> Hubbard's conclusion for To the Stars is quite another matter. At first glance it seemed that Part One was merely a prologue, so powerful by comparison was the conclusion. But in retrospect—a very short retrospect, true—the parts fit very well together, producing a whole preeminent worthiness. And because of its smoothness in delineation, its excellence in characterization and mood, its solidity of ideas, I do not hesitate, even at this short range, to classify it as good literature as well as excellent science fiction, deserving the posterity of hardcover publication.

To the Stars went on to achieve just such posterity, and was later published in Great Britain, Germany, Japan, Sweden, Denmark, France and Italy, a number of times in hardcover and usually in these foreign editions under the title Return to Tomorrow. Yet whatever the title, the story has left a lasting impact on the genre as pointed out by one of the field's most distinguished authors, Jerry Pournelle:

> To the Stars, by L. Ron Hubbard, is one of the greatest science fiction novels that has ever been written.

Ron wrote To the Stars circa May 1949, probably in Washington, D.C. And, during this period, he also wrote a number of other stories, including the final yarns in the famous Ole Doc Methuselah series, and "Beyond All Weapons."

Although "Beyond All Weapons" is considered by critics to be the pioneer story in modern science fiction for its original use of Einstein's time-dilation theory, *To the Stars*, published just a month later, is considered a much fuller development of the theme: "Seminal in scope, technical depth and influence," according to the official bibliographer of *The Fiction of L. Ron Hubbard*.

It was a theory Ron was intimately familiar with. When he had enrolled in the engineering school of The George Washington University (GWU) in the early 1930s, he had attended the first classes on nuclear physics, then called Atomic and Molecular Phenomena. Apparently, the claim to fame of the professor holding the chair of mathematics at the university was that supposedly he was one of only a few men in the entire country who understood Einstein's theory of relativity at the time. And as Ron related in the following anecdote, the man took himself quite seriously:

> I went in to see him one day to interview him for the college paper. I wanted him to tell me something about this theory of relativity this fellow Einstein was kicking around with and so forth. And I never had such sneers, contempt or was turned out on my ear quite so fast.

Still, Ron wrote his article.

> I said that one of only twelve people in the United States who understood Einstein was in the mathematics department of GW. I wrote this up as a very nice article, and then explained the Einstein theory in full so everybody understood it.
>
> Now, it wasn't that he never forgave me—he was so taken aback, he never dared speak to me crossly thereafter!

In *To the Stars* Ron expresses the time-dilation theme in this manner:

Space is deep, Man is small and Time is his relentless enemy.

And he continues by summarizing the problem in terms of an equation:

AS MASS APPROACHES INFINITY, TIME APPROACHES ZERO.

Two mathematicians derived the equations first—Lorentz and Fitzgerald. And a theoretical philosopher, Albert Einstein, showed its application. But if Lorentz and Fitzgerald and Einstein gave man his Solar System, they almost denied to him the stars.

Yet although tackling some of the ramifications of one of the primary scientific theories of our time, L. Ron Hubbard did what he had always done, ever since first entering the science fiction arena in 1938: he gave science fiction a human face, peopling it with real individuals struggling with real problems and facing real choices.

The power of *To the Stars* lies not only in its original approach to theme but in its characters—travelers on the "long passage" through time. Turn the page and prepare to meet them. First will come Alan Corday, a young and naive engineer-surveyor whose entire life is about to irrevocably change, and second, one of the most impenetrable and fascinating characters of modern science fiction, Captain Jocelyn, master of the *Hound of Heaven*. So belt yourself in and get ready for blastoff with these "people of the long passage."

The Editors

PROLOGUE

Space is deep, Man is small and Time is his relentless enemy.

In an ancient and forgotten age, he first discovered the barricade. Before space travel even began he knew the barricade was there. It was an equation. Without that equation, the basic equation of mass and time, man could not have progressed. But he did progress and he used fission and his mechanicians became mighty and his hopes large. But the terms of his salvation were the terms of his imprisonment as well.

AS MASS APPROACHES INFINITY, TIME APPROACHES ZERO.

Two mathematicians derived the equations first— Lorentz and Fitzgerald. And a theoretical philosopher, Albert Einstein, showed its application. But if Lorentz and Fitzgerald and Einstein gave man his Solar System, they almost denied to him the stars.

And yet, despite the difficulty derived by these

great men and confirmed first by nuclear physicists and then by actual use, there were still those who accepted and yet defied the law, a small cohort of ships and men who, throughout the ages, have kept the routes alive. The outcasts and pariahs of extra-atmosphere travel, the cursed and shunned by man, they coursed their lonely ways, far-bound but prisoners too, shackled fast by Time.

Knowing well their waiting fate, who would volunteer to become part of that thin group, knowing well their fate?

But amongst the societies of man there are always those who are outcasts from character or force of circumstance and there are adventurers who will not heed equations. And so the stars were reached and partially explored despite the fate of those who made the runs.

They called it the long passage, though it was not long—to the ship or its crew. It was only long to Earth. For those who approached the speed of light also approached the zero of time. At various high speeds the time differential upset men's lives. For they who lived weeks on the long passage left Earth and the Solar System to gather years in their absences.

The economic value of the long passage was small.

A six-week cruise to Alpha Centauri[†]—which had very little to give, unlike the further stars—brought back a crew to an Earth aged many years. Star commerce was not a venture of finance, it was only for the "benefit" of the crew.

Intersystem vessels could be geared to the high drive. And sometimes when port authorities waited with arrest, a liner would slip away from the gravity of the Sun and would lose itself to the stars. Or a criminal would steal a vessel in the hope of eclipsing years. But the results were the same.

He who is gone for a century cannot well return. He knows too little. His people are dead. He has no place and he does not fit. And what may have begun as an adventure for a crew invariably ended in the same way—another passage out, while behind them further age accumulated while the crew stayed young.

The only fraternity was within the ship.

The only hope was that someday someone might discover another equation, a solution to the barricade:

AS MASS APPROACHES THE SPEED OF LIGHT, TIME APPROACHES ZERO.

The outcasts of the long passage, those that stayed alive, never ceased to hope.

TO THE STARS

L. RON HUBBARD

3

[†] *Glossary included at back of book*

CHAPTER 1

Alan Corday stopped, momentarily blinded by the flash of a Mars-bound liner getting free from Earth. For an instant the skeletal racks had flashed red against the ink of sky and the one used now pulsated as it cooled. Corday did not like to be blinded here in this place, even for a moment. He wiped a tired hand against his blouse, carefully reassuring himself that his papers and wallet were still in place.

To the north glowed New Chicago, a broad humming city hiding beneath its five stages its hungry, its sick and its uncared-for lame. Civilization was mushroomed up from a mire; the columns were pretty, the fountains in the rich gardens played in many hues, cafes winked their invitations to the rich and under it all was the beggar's whine, a shrill, lost note, but steady enough to someday bring these towers down in wreck.

To an engineer-surveyor of the tenth class, New

Chicago was a grave in which he could bury all his years of school and field work for a pittance and eventually wander out of this life as poor as he had entered it. To an engineer tenth, people were polite because of his education and breeding, and distant because a man in need of a job must be poor.

He had heard vaguely that the new duke of Mars was employing men in public works and he knew certainly that an engineer tenth would be a rarity in that newness. But it took money to get to Mars unless one could work his way and Alan Corday had need to save his money.

In five years, her father had said, she could marry him, providing he had enough to start his own offices. Chica had wept a bit and he had tried to cheer her.

"They say there's work on Mars and that the new duke has an open hand. Don't cry, it won't be very long. I'll go for two years and two years will soon pass. Don't cry, honey. Please don't."

But two years would be long enough and five years were unthinkable. If his father had not seen fit to die a bankrupt— But it wasn't his father's fault. It was his own for dawdling his time away on special courses.

"Two years and I'll be home again, I swear it. Here,

look at me. Have I ever broken my word to you now? Have I? There. That's better. We'll make it yet—"

And he had painted a fine word picture for her of the house they'd have when he came back and how his purchased business would hum, and he had left her cheered. But he was not so sure himself. Mars was an uncertain place to go at best, even if the pay was high. And his going was even more uncertain now, for he had asked four ships so far this night and not one of them would haul without cash.

"You're a queer bird," the last captain had said. "What's a swell doing with a passage-beg? Thought you engineers was rolling in it."

What use to explain bankruptcy to this gnarled spaceman? Even the tenth class could go broke—and could retain its class standing providing it did not beg.

"Sell a couple of polo ponies and go cabin," the old skipper had said. "What's the world comin' to with a tenth class askin' to swab decks? Adventure ain't all it's cracked, sonny. You come for a lark. Go home and read a book."

Alan Corday felt the depth of the shadows now that the rocket afterglow was gone. It wasn't healthy here on the flats. He rubbed his knuckles nervously. He did not mind fighting but he had a job to do.

All the rebuffs he had received made him feel like a fool. A tenth class without two thousand for a passage was conspicuous. He wished he had worn dungarees and that he had sometime learned to lie. But a gentleman didn't lie and, broke or not, he was still a gentleman.

Lights flickered unevenly through the filter of a garbage-strewn alley. He was getting down near the stews now, out of the officers' neighborhood. He didn't have a gun and he was a fine target for a footpad in this white silk jacket. But he picked his way toward the lights.

A black cat leaped with a startled squall from his path, crossed it and vanished; Alan laughed nervously at the way the sudden noise had made his hand shake. Jumping from a cat!

Then he heard the first notes of the melody. Strange, eerie notes, haunting and terrible, were being plucked from an ancient piano—slow music, simple and yet complex. One could expect many things on the flats, he had been led to believe by a lurid press, but not a melody like that. Alan knew something of music but he had never heard such a thing before. The floating notes were like a magnet and without knowing that he had moved he found himself standing outside a cheap glass building looking intently at the door.

It was just a common stew. A drunk lay sprawled on the walk, the side of his head covered with blood, a series of snores wheezing between his teeth. And over him floated the eerie song.

Alan stepped into the yellow light and thrust back the door. Because of its stillness he had expected to find the place empty of all but the player. But below a bluish haze which crawled twixt ceiling and floor, a jammed mass of men sat hushed, their drinks arrested in their hands.

It was tribute, Alan thought, and certainly the music was of a quality to do this even amongst such a crew as this. But then he saw they were not listening. They were waiting and they were afraid.

Far across the reeking place sat the player, engrossed in his moving hands, oblivious of any audience. The piano was battered and chipped with blasts; three members of a string orchestra, almost equally misused, crouched with the rest of the room, waiting and afraid. And the young man played.

He was a strange young man. In this bluish light his face looked too sharp, too white, too handsome. There were strange qualities mingled in that face, raptness uppermost now. A helmet and spaceman's gloves lay to hand on the piano top. A shirt and trousers, startlingly white, gave no clue to any age but certainly not to this. And about the young man's waist was a wide belt of gold metal from which hung a weapon Alan had never seen before. And the room waited, hushed.

The hands strayed for the final notes and then hung in memory of the melody dying away now in the strings. Then the young man stood and Alan saw that he was not young. Gradually the reverie left his face, gradually other expressions began to combine in it. The man was nearing fifty and his eyes were hard. His mouth was cynical and his whole thin face was cruel. But he was handsome to the point of beauty, handsome and diamond hard.

The proprietor cringed up to him. "Your worship . . . may we serve again . . . the men—"

The man swept down a languid, cynical eye and then stepped from the musicians' platform. He knew what he had done to them. And he knew he had done it with music. His smile told that, if a smile it was.

"Bucko!" he said. And a burly, gray-haired man jumped eagerly up. "Have their cups full. Yes, and let them drink to the *Hound of Heaven*."

The gray-haired one spoke and the place shook and yet one could tell that he thought he spoke softly. "Fill up! Fill up and drink to Captain Jocelyn! Jocelyn and the *Hound of Heaven*. Ah, no you won't!" he hastily added, grabbing a spaceman who had sought to dive for the door. The spaceman turned, caught a blow on the mouth and crumpled into a chair. The burly one beamed at him.

"Fill up and drink!" shouted a blowsy girl.

"And who's this?" said the man who had played, looking with something like interest at Alan.

"Two more rounds!" said the burly one with an amiable roar. "And then we'll open the books for your names. Right ones or wrong ones, but by Jupe you better sign!"

Another spaceman tried to get away and a slip of a girl in a queen's finery tripped him before he could make it.

"Sit down," said the man who had played, seating himself carelessly near the entrance. "I'm Jocelyn."

"Alan Corday," said Alan, guardedly extending a hand. But if Jocelyn saw it he ignored it.

"A tenth class by your jacket," said Jocelyn. "Drink?"

"Ah . . . no, thank you. I—" He steadied himself with an inward rage. A space captain refusing the hand of a tenth class. And making the tenth class feel self-conscious and confused in the bargain.

"Are you going to Mars?" said Alan.

Jocelyn filled a two-ounce jigger and shoved it across the table. "Drink up."

Alan was on the verge of refusal. But there was something in Jocelyn's being which reached out and entangled Alan's will. Confused, he drank.

"Educated as what?" said Jocelyn.

"Engineer-surveyor," said Alan, reaching for his papers.

Jocelyn waved the offered sheaf aside. "Ever been in space?"

"Why, no, but I feel I might—"

"How old are you?"

"Twenty-six."

"You're a child," said Jocelyn. "And you are also a fool. What are you doing here on the flats at this hour? Kill somebody?"

"Sir, I—"

"Sit down!" said Jocelyn. "Answer me!"

"It's a private matter."

"Ah, a girl. You were indiscreet—"

"Confound your tongue!" said Alan hotly. "My father was bankrupted and I am going to Mars to serve the duke if I can. This is honorable enough, isn't it?"

"And when you've served two years?" said Jocelyn.

"I'll come back and reestablish my firm and marry—" He stopped. He had not meant to bring her into this. And then, out of his own embarrassment, he saw that Jocelyn had death in his eyes.

Struck without warning, Alan went down into the sawdust. He came up from the overturned chair, both hands snatching for Jocelyn's throat. And then two men had him from behind and there was a knife a quarter of an inch already into his ribs.

"Put him back," said Jocelyn. "You young fool. Drink this up and go home." And his hand shook as he poured the liquor and it spilled over to become a black pool on the ringed table.

But Alan would not be set free so easily and the men held fast. In a moment he felt the indignity of further struggle and stood straight. The burly one was at hand now beside Jocelyn.

"Hello!" he roared. "A tenth class! Or so I been told

your collar tabs so mean. Well, you'll make a fine addition! A fine addition! Educated too, huh? What's he educated in, Skipper?"

"Engineer-surveyor," said Jocelyn coldly. "But he's not going."

"Well, I'm blessed if I know what that is," said the burly one, "but it do sound like he might be taught one end of a celestolabe from t'other. Built nice, too. You'll like the *Flea Circus*, young-un."

"I said he wasn't going!" snapped Jocelyn.

"Shucks, Skipper. You'n me, watch on watch while these logheads ride in comfort and security, and here's a fine second mate—"

"I'll sign if you're going to Mars," said Alan.

Jocelyn looked at him in deep contempt.

"Mars, why sure. Sign to Mars. Gow-eater, take your slimy paws off that young-un and get the articles."

Jocelyn got up, swept the filled glass into his hand and drained it. He reached back of him as though he had eyes there and seized the unresisting girl who had earlier tripped the spaceman. He brought her close to him, deliberately forgetting Alan. But the girl was looking and her eyes were dreamy and veiled.

"Sign fifteen," said Jocelyn. "And hold the rest. We clear at midnight. Understood?"

"You bet your life," said the burly one.

Jocelyn pulled the girl out through the door and called at a cruising hack. "Some place they sell fancy clothes," Alan heard him say.

And he looked down and saw his name on the articles. "The *Hound of Heaven*. Outward Bound for Alpha Centauri, Betelgeuse and Other Ports of Call." He went white and lunged back. But Gow-eater and his friend still had him.

"Now, now," said the burly one, "you'll get to Mars someday."

"You can't hold me!" shouted Alan. "You can't do it! *You're on the long passage!*"

The burly one grinned. "I'm Bucko Hale, sonny. You wouldn't be here if you wasn't desperate. So why get desperate about the long passage? Who knows, ten or fifteen years we might even come back. That's Earth time. But you won't be much older. Now calm—"

"Let me go!" screamed Alan, half an inch of knife already trying to pin him to the wall. "Let me go!" And there was real frenzy in him now, knife or no knife. He knew all about the Lorentz-Einstein Relativity Equations. He knew what happened when a ship got to ninety-nine percent of the speed of light. And his girl—

Bucko Hale reached out and struck him, struck him expertly and well, and the Gow-eater put a belt around his arms and body.

"No need to attrac' a patrol," said Bucko. "Now the rest of you boys step up and sign and we'll have a merry time. Wine, women and billions, me boys, and a nice, long look at history . . ."

CHAPTER 2

He knew many things but his condition was close to delirium and the things he knew merged with the things he feared until his mind was a seething maelstrom of nightmare.

Buckled down tight in a hard steel bunk, he could see only shadows and the dim meshes of the springs overhead and these blurred into symbols and figures and spun.

The pages of Einstein's text fluttered in his head and the symbols of Einstein's work danced before his eyes. What he had once considered as a curious and rather interesting phenomenon he now saw in its ghastly truth.

Cold, dispassionate hand of science, how glibly it could write! "When the velocity of mass approaches one hundred eighty-six thousand miles per second, time approaches zero; as mass approaches one hundred eighty-six thousand miles per second it approaches infinity." They had discovered that years and years ago and it had stood, the barricade to the long passage; and Alan saw it now with nightmare clarity. Time approaches zero, time approaches zero, time approaches zero.

Three weeks to Alpha Centauri at one hundred eighty thousand miles per second! "As mass approaches infinity, time approaches zero *for the mass*." Three weeks to Alpha Centauri *for the mass*. For the mass!

"But time is constant at finite speeds." At finite speeds! And that meant Earth. That meant New Chicago. And that meant the woman who might have become his wife.

The pages fluttered in his brain and the figures blurred in his sight and he quailed before it as had quailed the hardest and least sensitive of men. He was on the long passage with the outcasts and pariahs of space. And from the ache in his body he knew he was already split away from the clocks of Earth and on a deadly route of his own.

He knew little about these people of the long passage beyond an occasional account in a newspaper, beyond an occasional display in a museum, beyond a new bauble in a store. But his own ability to take care of himself with them he did not greatly doubt. Not yet. He was thinking of a girl and a promise and his heart gave a sick wrench within him.

She would wait. He knew she would wait, for he had loved her long and since childhood he had been her guidon—

Something stuck him in the arm and he glanced, startled, to find a ruddy face, haloed with gray, close by him.

"Hello! Awake again? Now, now, calm down, young fellow. They say you'll be second mate and I'm to take care of you. So steady as she goes and sheer off the asteroids, eh?"

Alan spoke thickly: "Go to the devil."

"Dare say we'll meet, but neither of us are in a hurry. The devil gets enough from Time-Zero." He laughed with delight at his own pleasantry and repeated it, "The devil gets his fill from Time-Zero." This cheered him so much that he had to skip backwards and turn a whirl. Then he peered, very close and solemn, at Alan. "I'm Dr. Strange. You weren't on dope or anything were you when you ran away?"

"I didn't run away! I'm here from no choice!"

"Don't want to kill you. Compound Theta Seven won't work on opium. Fights it. Kills the patient. Wanted to be sure. But you're to be second when you come around. Bad case. Hard to work."

The ship was completely silent with only a faint vibration in her. And the sound of footfalls rang clear as Jocelyn approached. He ignored Alan, looking instead at the berths across the room. Alan saw now that he was in a sick bay and that he was not alone. Fifteen others were strapped in their tiers.

Jocelyn surveyed the berths and gave a faint snort of contempt. "Shabby enough. But I need a phoneman for second con. Jar one up; be quick."

Strange altered his face quickly. He was anxious. "Aye, aye, Skipper." And he snatched a needle from a kit held out to him by a child Alan had not seen before. This grave-faced orderly was not more than eight; his hair was cropped, a clean streak showed around his mouth and his medical jacket got under his feet, having been meant for a man.

The doctor jabbed a spaceman in the opposite berth and the man began to toss.

Apologetically, the doctor said, "I can't guarantee his health, Captain. I tried to work them over but some of them are tough. Resistant. This young man," and he indicated Alan, "won't trace at all. He merely raves—"

Jocelyn fixed a hard eye on Strange and his handsome face turned a little paler. "Then you were drunk yesterday."

"Me? Why, Skipper—!"

"You *were* drunk," said Jocelyn, talking quieter as his anger rose. "I told you to leave his mind alone! What do I care what happens to these cattle. But you've got a trained brain there. Leave it alone! You fool, will you dabble with your confounded hypnosis—" He quieted himself with an effort. "Leave his mind alone, Doctor. Psychiatry or no, there's much you have to learn about men."

Strange hastily began to excuse himself but Jocelyn cut him off.

"Unstrap him," said Jocelyn, pointing to the awakened spaceman.

The doctor quickly began on the buckles and Alan, like an animal in a trap, ranged his eyes over the room for a means of escape. There was a door at either end and one in the side. But the one in the side was marked Emergency and its handles plainly indicated that it was not lightly to be touched, for they were massive wheels.

Alan wondered if it were part of the damage control system which must exist on such a craft. He speculated that it might lead to a lifeboat compartment and if it did— Hope began to stir up in him.

The spaceman was also staring about. He was a blond youngster, marked with a ray burn across his forehead and marked as well with the pallor peculiar to space. He had been on the Venusian run for five years, comfortable if dangerous, ten thousand miles an hour, a week in port at either end. A trifle different from the long passage. And the hard desperation which had begun to set his face showed how well he knew it.

But he was cunning. He permitted himself to be steadied to his feet and then bent as if he would test his limbs after their confinement. But he came up with a powerful blow of each hand, striking Jocelyn a heavy backhand in the chest and throwing the doctor aside like a sack. There was a blazing insanity in his face, caused half by drugs, half by his terror, and even while Jocelyn staggered, the spaceman lunged for the emergency port. Behind it there might be a lifeboat. Beyond it might lie freedom.

And his big hands wrenched at the locks and spun them open, one, two and three. His grip was resting on the fourth and last when the sick bay resounded with the lash of an arc pistol.

Alan stared. The spaceman stood immobile for a breath and then his hands fell away from the last wheel. He stumbled back, drifting with the acceleration of the ship, clutched a stanchion and with a mild, apologetic look, crumpled to the floor, dead.

Jocelyn gathered himself up from the filthy deck. He was breathing heavily from the blow and the ionized, discolored air around his drawn weapon seemed to pulse as though he breathed out smoke.

He went to the door to close the locks. Air was seeping out of the compartment, sucked greedily by outer space.

He came back and holstered his gun.

"Get me another one up, Doctor."

Gnomelike and nervous, Dr. Strange hung on the edges of bunks, now here, now there, needle ready, his thin voice sawing the silence while gravely near him stood the urchin with his jacket from chin to floor.

It was a process Alan was to find common and necessary on the long passage—psychotherapy. Brutal therapy. Nothing delicate about it. If you had to take a man's mind half away to make him useful on a ship, take it away. Crush his memories, rob his personality, stamp out his rebellion. There wasn't much time that could be spent, drugs were cheap and crewmen were dear. Narcohypnosis was the most effective speed tool. A vessel on the long passage was never full complement and a man made into an idiot, if he could steer, was better than a full personality with revolt in his heart.

Despite the captain's injunctions, Alan twice awoke out of a groggy doze to find the red-faced doctor close by his ear. Once Alan got his arm free after many a cunning twist. He grabbed Strange by the throat and would have killed him if the man's needle had not been half full and close by.

"No hard feelings," said the doctor much later, coming back from a patient. "And you're in no danger from me." He laughed. "I'm curious about your society and age, about what a tenth class might be. And I thought you might have had a lecture or two on your modern psychiatry stashed away in your cranium. Got drunk and couldn't get a book this time. I'm very seldom drunk but once in a while when you come back and see things changed you want to drink." He underwent a change of expression and averted his eyes. But in a moment he was bouncing again and laughing.

"They're smarter now. But that's to be expected. They get smarter and smarter and learn new things. So you're safe. When I was a boy they had just invented the Weaver cellular exhaustion technique. I— What's the matter?"

Alan was looking at him in despair. "How old are you?"

The doctor shrugged. "Fifty, sixty ship-years. *Flea Circus* years. That's ship slang. We call her the *Flea Circus*. We—"

"What year were you born?" demanded Alan.

The doctor sheered off. "Guess you better sleep now. Day or two the skipper will want—"

"The Weaver exhaustion technique is three thousand years or more old!" said Alan. "How old are you? Not ship-years! Earth-years! How old are you?"

The doctor cringed. But he was instantly himself. "You don't need to worry about your wits. They've learned a lot and all I wanted was what you might know. I'm a very nosy fellow. But you won't talk and now I understand why and so you're safe enough, Jocelyn or no. I'll have to tell him. They evidently proof a tenth class when they're born. There's no sentient period behind what proofing they gave you. You can't take a hypnotic suggestion and you won't reply. I'll have to tell Jocelyn. That will surprise him. Very, very interesting. What they must have intended you for with all the trouble they've taken on you. A tenth class—"

"Look," said Alan, "beyond basic lectures in social intercourse I was never trained in your field. I know nothing beyond the fact that all noble-born children are proofed. I am an engineer by training, and building a bridge and breaking a mind are two different things. Leave me alone."

He turned his face to the scarred wall.

Outward bound on the long passage, outward bound to the stars. He did not know the speed of this pariah nor how close it would come to light. If it was as slow as ninety-four percent it still meant that for every moment ticked by the clocks of the *Hound of Heaven*, hundreds passed on Earth. *If the* Hound *spent six weeks in a round trip to Alpha Centauri, nine years would pass on Earth.*

"As mass approaches the speed of light, time approaches zero." It was his sentence. A cold equation, a dispassionate mathematics, but it was Alan Corday's sentence to forever.

The run to Alpha Centauri would be the shortest trip they could make.

How old would be his people when he saw them next? How old?

CHAPTER 3

A fourteen-year-old girl, nervous and frightened, eyes staring, sidled into the sick bay. She made two or three efforts to talk and then sang out with a rush:

"Cap'n's compliments and Corday's wanted on the bridge and he better make it snappy."

She gulped and subsided. Strange came up from his narrow white desk and hurriedly began to unlash his patient, talking cheerily the while.

"What's the course, Snoozer? You always have the latest. Whither bound? Or do I have to produce some candy?"

"Cap'n told me not to talk."

"How about a cognac bonbon?" said Strange.

She gulped hard, her gaze fascinated by the doctor, standing first on one foot and then the other as she watched.

"*Two* cognac bonbons," said Strange. "Snoozer's the

captain's runner," he explained to Alan as he helped his charge sit up.

"Two?" faltered Snoozer, wiping a hand across her mouth.

Alan stood unsteadily. The girl was very pretty, would be more so if she ever washed her face or combed her hair.

Strange looked fixedly at Alan. "Now you'll be good, won't you?" And taking silence for an answer walked away to his desk to unlock a drawer. He pulled out a box of candy and was in the act of removing the cover when the girl managed a decision.

"No. You'll know soon enough," she said, looking forlornly at the bonbons and suddenly conscious of a bruise on her wrist which she began to nurse. She let out a shuddering sigh and abandoned the offered box.

Making sure that Alan was following, she darted back through the doorway, gave the bonbons one last look of despair and then led off up a ladder.

Alan braced himself. For a long time now he had been running over what he meant to say to Jocelyn and the approaching interview quickened his breath and pace.

Running on ahead, the girl would sometimes stop

to make sure he was still coming. Alan was. But his eyes were searching as he went for lifeboats. He knew that a space lifeboat could span back the short distance to Earth and he was sure that he could run one. But as he went, though he saw many things, he found no sign of an air-lock berthing.

Such was his state of mind that few details registered with him. He was gazing on this vessel as a very temporary prison and he was little interested in her. Vaguely it came to him that she was a complicated ship, multidecked, every inch of space used, and that she was manned by a very strange crew.

Those people he saw were off duty, for his course lay wholly within the berthing compartments and mess halls. What surprised him most was the number of children, for he saw some dozens of them playing on the decks or cradled in the berths. One woman looked at him curiously and said something to a dozing man in the next berth after he had passed.

In the mess hall some card games were in progress and one group was listening raptly to an old man who was telling them a tale. There were more women than men here and it was puzzling until one realized that half the company of the vessel was on duty elsewhere.

A companionway led upwards from the mess hall and here Snoozer halted again to wait. A scrawled sign over her head said Bridge Country.

Alan stopped for a moment to gather his wits and suddenly felt a presence behind him. It was the gangling, pasty man that had held him in the dive, Gow-eater. And Alan knew that he had had a silent guard all the way.

"Let's go," said Gow-eater.

Alan mounted the ladder and found himself staring through a thick double port at the blackness of space and the blazing stars.

"In there," said Snoozer in a frightened whisper and Alan turned to an open door.

The chart room was ancient in design, having a globe for the plotting of courses and cases for the three-dimensional charts, a ledge for computation and two magnetic-legged stools. Jocelyn, helmet pushed up and back, white shirt open at the throat, sat with a pair of compasses idly making holes in a pad.

A torrent of speech was ready on Alan's lips but Jocelyn began to talk without looking up, his presence effectually silencing the younger man.

"Mr. Corday, I've had you up to show you duty. Sit down on that stool and keep your mouth closed. You have a lot to learn."

Alan hesitated and then spoke angrily.

"Captain Jocelyn, you seem to have decided that I would do a lot of things. I do not intend to do them. You have taken me, without my consent, into a rotten life. I dare say you consider yourself very well above the law. But let me promise you, before we go further, that the first port into which we call will find me before the authorities bringing charges for kidnaping. I have no intention—"

Jocelyn looked up and his mouth curled. "You are a fool, Corday. Sit down."

Alan stiffened. He was unaccustomed to scorn or contempt and the look and tone of the man drove his temper to a higher beat. On the table lay the captain's gun and belt, coiled amid pens and charts. A little whiter, Alan made as if to sit down and then with a swift strike snatched the butt of the gun.

Instantly the sharp-pointed compasses came up and stabbed. They bore straight through muscle and bone and pinned Alan's hand to the chart board, points penetrating all the way through and half an inch deep into the wood.

In the agony of it Alan struck with his free fist, wrenching at his imprisoned hand the while. Jocelyn deflected the blow and struck back. Alan reeled and slumped, held up only by the impaling compasses.

"Corday," said Jocelyn, "you have a lot to learn." But he looked different for a moment, his eyes probing hopefully into the slack face of the younger man. Then he wrenched out the compasses and reached over to boost Alan to the stool.

Sullenly Alan bound up his bleeding hand with a handkerchief. The gun butt still extended toward him and now and then his eyes flicked to it.

"You are young," said Jocelyn. "You've got a lot of romantic nonsense in you about the freedom of the individual. You're filled to the eyes with the importance of your own petty concerns. I have rescued you from something worse than this and I'm not paid. You are a fool. Self-conscious, quixotic, short on experience, crammed with undigested learning. I am doing you the honor of offering you a post of responsibility. My advice to you is that you accept."

Alan glowered at him.

Jocelyn flung a hand at the untidy masses of charts. "You are an engineer of the tenth class. You have been eugenically selected for brains and trained to empire building. Probably your family lost its money—and I saw that they did not forgive that in your age. You need money. We are outward bound on a short cruise, a few weeks—"

"Do me the honor of not lying," said Alan.

"You know something about this, then?"

"Too much."

"Like you to assume you know a great deal when you don't. What have they taught you in school, the latest?"

"And why would you be interested in that?"

Jocelyn looked at him contemptuously. "Do you suppose, Mr. Corday, that I enjoy, that anyone on this ship enjoys, the fate of the long passage? Do you think that we want this sentence to continue forever? Are you such a fool as to believe that people in such ships as this have no hope of a country, a society, of belonging?

"What are we?" he cried in sudden rage. "Outcasts. Pariahs. We land and are gone a few weeks in our lives and we return to find that years have stripped away everything we have left. On a normal fifty-light-year voyage, a century can pass on Earth. And what happens in a century, Mr. Corday? We age in weeks on the long passage. Earth and the Universe ages by decades. And who wants us? Who will be there when we return? What government? What technologies? We bring back wealth from the stars to the descendants of those who commissioned us. We speak archaic tongues more ancient on every trip. Our learning is nothing and in any society we would misfit and starve and we're outward bound again. Do you know what it is to be without a country, Mr. Corday? Without people? Without a home? Who cares what happens to us? We have this little hell of a ship. Not even another engaged on the long passage can be our friend. We are out of time, out of step. We are nothing!

"Ponder if you want the joy of seeing the centuries crush and destroy whatever we leave behind us. It's an empty sight, Mr. Corday. We are hated and we do not belong."

He had stood up as he talked and his face was whiter with strain. He slumped back now and from the cabinet behind him took a bottle. He poured a brimming glass and into it poured a powder from a folded paper. He drank without relish and set it back.

"Now what are the latest time equations, Mr. Corday?"

Alan was confused by this difference of character and overwhelmed by the graphic details of the fate which was now his. But he could enjoy the cruelty of what he had to say as revenge against what had been done to him.

"There are no new time equations, Captain Jocelyn."

There was a long silence and then Jocelyn, as though nothing had occurred, picked up a sheaf of chart changes and began to finger them.

"Mr. Corday, if you perform duty faithfully in the next three or four months, you will return to Earth with a large fortune. It is possible that less than fifty years Earth time will have elapsed. You are an educated man. There is much that is very antiquated aboard this ship and much that you can remedy with your newer technology. The Hound of Heaven is not a very old ship, less than sixty years ship time. She was well designed for her period but that is two millenniums past. You are here, you cannot help it. I would advise you to make the best of your situation."

Alan looked bleakly at the black heavens and the blazing stars. He was stunned even though he had known. Half a century. Half a century. How old would his girl be then?

And she would wait.

Numbly he got up from the stool and fumbled his
way down the ladder. He turned once and looked back.
Captain Jocelyn was emptying a paper into a brimming
drink.

Listen

to the Unforgettable Music of *To the Stars*

A breathtakingly original tone poem—inspired by L. Ron Hubbard's science fiction masterpiece—brilliantly composed by Chick Corea and performed by the Elektric Band. novel of a perilous future when the first starships leap the galaxy at nearly the speed of light, leaving their pioneering crews essentially untouched—but exiled—by the passage of time while whole generations vanish

The massive sweep, scope, power and vivid human drama of one of the greatest novels in the history of science fiction—L. Ron Hubbard's *To the Stars*—has been captured by 12-time Grammy award-winning Chick Corea and his famed Elektric Band in a superbly imaginative tone poem that spectacularly breaks new musical ground.

Richly portrayed musically are indelible scenes, events and characters in Hubbard's forever on Earth. With mankind's greater destiny among the stars held in the cosmic balance, Corea's virtuoso musical journey weaves melodies, rhythms and tonal moods into what has been acclaimed as an unrivaled technical and creative triumph.

Let the groundbreaking music of the album inspired by *To the Stars* help speed your voyage through space and time and the wonders of the universe.

ORDER YOUR COPY TODAY!
Orders sent within 24 hours of receipt.

Please send me _____ copies of *To the Stars* CD by Chick Corea and the Elektric Band.
Retail Price: U.S.$20.00*   Can$28.00
*California residents add 8.25% sales tax.   Shipping: $2.00   TOTAL:_____

Credit Card Number (American Express, Visa, MC, Discover) _____

Expiration Date _____   *Signature* _____

Name _____

Address _____

City _____   *State/Province* _____   *Zip/Postal Code* _____

Phone (day) _____   *Phone (evening)* _____

E-mail address _____

Phone Toll Free:1-877-8GALAXY   Fax:1-323-466-7817
E-mail: sales@galaxypress.com   Online: www.tothestars.com
Galaxy Music, 7051 Hollywood Boulevard, Suite 200, Hollywood, CA 90028

BUSINESS REPLY MAIL
FIRST-CLASS MAIL   PERMIT NO. 75738   LOS ANGELES CA

POSTAGE WILL BE PAID BY ADDRESSEE

GALAXY PRESS
7051 HOLLYWOOD BLVD
LOS ANGELES CA 90028-9771

CHAPTER 4

He sat in the second mate's cabin giving an apathetic ear to the Deuce. On the desk before him spread the master plans of the vessel, much chewed by cockroaches and dimmed with mold and overlaid time after time with smudged pencil marks which showed a multiplicity of changes.

"Yer see," said the Deuce, "she's altered around somewhat every trip or two. That's yer penalty fer spannin' time so. Yer gets obsolete ever time yer hits port. An if yer lucky and the devils ain't terrin' Earth apart with er war or if yer ain't got a dictator or if yer just plain suffered in the docks yer gets some changes made."

He was a small man, an ideal spaceman from the standpoint of weight. His jaw bulged with tobacco and his eyes bulged with the concentration of speech. He swallowed the juice. His cap was a battered something with "Chief Engineer" in tarnished gold on it and his black dungarees carried the white, smudged lettering *"Martian Girl."*

"So the old lady don't get any break to speak of," he continued. "Me, I'm really an instrument man and I guess I could fix anything if it was small, but I don't belong at what I'm doin'. Shortage of talent. So I don't give her no break either. Burned her topside drives to cinders last trip through not knowing and had to work for two days in the icebox. That's 'outside.' So deck force construction ain't tended to whatever and I guess there's a mort of gimmicks yer could wrangle around and get right."

Alan looked dully at the plans. He was only half hearing what the Deuce was saying.

"Not that she ain't a bad hooker. Yer couldn't find er better one for the long passage. Her hull's a beauty. Shieldite. Solid. She come along about four, five hundred years after the first metal was poured together that would insulate gammas. And they went whole hog and no holds barred and by golly they built yer whole ship of it. Made her for the military it says there under yer thumb and they still got gun emplacements eround and they used to be a lot of signal lights strung up on her bows. Fancy. Admirals walked her bridge, they tell me.

"Then she went out to Alpha on a expedition. Tell me the guvmunt, whichever one it was, did things when she was a young ship. Anyway yer old baby was obsolete when she come back. She'd missed Alpha and her crew was half gone and the rest had mutinied. And there was yer ship, fifty years out of date and only five years old. Somebody bought her for scrap for a small pile of Gs but they put a high drive in her instead, she already havin' been equipt for the long passage, and *they* tried fer Alpha. Nine years they figured and come back with a fortune. But yer know what happens. Alpha ain't got any fortunes and never did have and greed took them farther and yer crew came home to people they didn't know . . . well, we won't talk about that. But yer see the mess she's in."

He got rid of his cud and gnawed another one from the verminous plug he kept in his hip pocket. When he got this going he pointed a solid finger at the steering diagrams.

"They ain't built anything like that they tell me in two thousand Earth-years and it's been renewed once. That's yer department, Mr. Corday. Bulkheads, berthings and the steering. Bridge instruments and communications. Yer got a full bill. But that there steerin' is what yer need to start on first. Last trip we went appetite over tincup when we hit an atmosphere in Rigel Kentaurus. Bashed things up. So yer got a hurry job and they'll thank yer handsome."

The Deuce looked expectantly at the bottle, Alan's liquor ration, which perched on the desk and then, being unable to communicate the hint, swung his leg down from the arm of the chair and stood up.

"When yer got it figured I'll send up a couple welders." He looked uncomfortably at Alan, not sure that he had been heard at all now. Then he shrugged. "Well, good luck."

He had been gone for some time when Alan realized he was no longer there and talking. The antiquity of these plans. And yet they were drawn only fifty or sixty ship-years ago. And the spelling was so ancient that it almost required a linguist to translate.

He became aware of someone at the door and looked up with a start. She had been standing there for some time, poised and indolent, looking at him, her eyes soft, a little taunting. He recognized the girl in the dive.

She was wearing new clothes, clothes designed to show what they were supposed to hide. He knew her suddenly through and through. She knew a great deal. And she was lovely and knew that as well.

"Hello," she said.

Alan stood up out of manners.

"I am Mistress Luck and you are the captain's new mate. Ah, what a beastly little room they've given you and the whole sixth deck as empty as a drum."

Her perfume reached him and a sudden aching nostalgia took him. Gardenias. Gardenias and a ball and New Chicago.

"Not even a sheet on your bunk. Poor boy. Stay right there, I'll be back."

He did stay there, standing, eyes turned to what he had left behind him, his heart beating unevenly, his brain whirling again as it had almost ceaselessly since his misadventure. How old would Chica be when he saw her once again? How old?

She mustn't wait! She mustn't. But she would be happy for two years and hopeful. Then she would worry a little for three. And at last she would have to assume that he was dead. The long passage would never occur to her. It was not too well known. The ships which returned were few and new ones seldom joined the strange trade. She mustn't wait. And yet fear told him that she would. And the years would pass by—

Mistress Luck was pouring him a stiff drink. "Now you mustn't neglect your rations. That keeps a man going, keeps him from thinking. You don't want to think, you silly boy. Why think? The Universe is broad."

He looked into the amber fluid and heard her behind him, making up his bunk. And then he looked up and saw Jocelyn.

It was not strange that Jocelyn should be there, for this was only a step from the bridge.

"Hard at work, I see," said Jocelyn.

Alan stood up, sullen.

"Come, my dear," said Jocelyn. "I've a thing or two to be done."

The girl deliberately finished the bunk and then gave Alan a slow look. "Don't let them abuse you, fellow. When you want something, sing out and make them step. Hasn't he told you you're third in command?"

Jocelyn twitched at his belt. "Mr. Corday, it is part of my lady's duties to see that officers' country is comfortable. She takes many privileges. But not too comfortable, Mr. Corday."

Alan flushed to his hair roots.

"And," said Jocelyn, letting the girl step into the passage, "not third in command, Mr. Corday. That's earned and you haven't earned it. Shall we go, my dear?"

He escorted the girl along the passage and to his own quarters. Their door slammed and there was silence.

Alan had stepped out of his door to watch them go and the heavy voice behind him startled him.

"Well, well, sonny. So you run afoul of that."

He turned to find a woman. She was heavily, even magnificently, dressed and she had ropes of pearls around her throat. Her voice was husky, cigar husky, and the wreathing smoke of a black cheroot coiled around her face. Her white, lardulous flesh fell over itself in rolls and she was old. But her eyes were young and there was coquetry in her voice. Alan shuddered.

"Ask yourself what happened to our old second mate, Mr. Corday. And then think about a lot of things. Well, aren't you asking me in?"

"By all means," said Alan swiftly.

She settled herself in his chair and took up his unfinished drink, looking archly at him. "Seems to me you have a lot to learn, Mr. Corday."

"So people find time to tell me."

"And it's true enough. What do you want with a woman like that? Takes experience to know what a man wants. Lots of experience, Mr. Corday. Blah, issue liquor! I'll have Marby bring you something easier on the palate. Marby's my friend. They're all my friends, Mr. Corday, even the ones the sawbones drove daffy. I suppose you're wondering who the devil I am."

"To be frank, I was."

"Well, to be frank, I'm Queen. There are a hundred and twenty souls in the *Fleu Circus* this trip. But there's only one Queen."

"I dare say you're married to some gentleman aboard?"

She laughed and laughed and looked at him and laughed again. And then, with another solid slug from the bottle wheezed, "Oh, that's rich. Who'd ever have thought of it."

"I did not know I was so witty," said Alan.

"You ain't witty, son. You're just a little green. You got any idea what the turnover is in the stars?" She gradually subsided and for a moment was serious. In a flat voice she said, "I had a man once. Married true and square. But he's dead these ten ship-years.

Jerry Boanne. You ever hear of Jerry Boanne? But you wouldn't. That's hundreds of years before you was born. Skipper he was of the *King's Lion*, Earth to Venus, Venus to Earth, and then he took what didn't belong to him, a hundred million in gold, and he hit the long passage. Well, the devil with it. It's over and last trip I couldn't even find his grave. There was a city on it. Would have amused Jerry. Buildin' a city on his bones. You got any cigars? No? I'll have Marby bring you some cigars. He's a bad cook but he's my friend. They're all my friends. And you, too, Mr. Corday. Now to business."

Alan began, "I am sure—"

"Oh no, you're not, sonny." And she surged forward, glanced up and down the passage and closed the door. It was a bare room but it had a desk and several shadowed corners; she made certain they housed no microphones. Then she began to speak, rapidly and low.

"Kid, you're sick. I know. And you didn't ask to be here."

"That I did not," said Alan.

"Kid, you're the first chance we've had."

An electric thrill of expectancy crackled through him.

"You don't know Jocelyn yet," she continued harshly.

"You may think you do but you don't. He's rotten, rotten clear through. Behind that handsome face there's brimstone burning. Few of us are here from choice. But we haven't had a chance."

"What are you talking about?" he said, matching her low tones.

"Let's not sport around, sonny. You want to get home?"

"I've got to!"

"Okay, sonny. You're a tenth class. You can cover a lot in courts. You belong to a period that's still alive back there. You can navigate a ship because you've got education. You can make it smooth for us when we arrive."

"Wait. I haven't any power back there. I'm a noble, yes. But when the money is gone the title goes. You—"

"Devil take the money. There's millions loose in this old hooker. Money's nothing to us, any of us. See these pearls? They're worth a hundred thousand. Well, blink but they are. And there's the most of us that's sick of this. We want to go back, not to live in these metal walls anymore, to have a chance. And you've got to help us."

"That's mutiny!"

"Call it an ugly word if you like. There's no law in the long passage but a captain and captains come and go. They come and go, kid. You understand me? And there's only one way to go on the long passage."

"If you mean murder—"

"More ugly words. Call it murder. You won't get spattered. Will you play?"

He hesitated.

"Don't be a fool!" she said hoarsely. "You want home. You've got a dame waiting. I can tell."

"What will I have to do?"

"That's better." She sank back and crossed her fat legs. "You can't run this hooker yet and she can't be turned in midflight the way she's rigged. Her steering assembly, accordin' to the Deuce, is about ready to cave in. You want to get home?"

"Yes!"

"All right. You stand by. We'll take care of all the details. Don't let on to the crew you know. There's plenty that are in but some there are that ain't and you don't know them. You're an officer. You can stand off. Don't look for no signs, for if Jocelyn knew this—" She made an expressive motion with her hand.

"Now for details," she continued. "In about two

minutes European you bone up on everything you got to know to swing us back to Earth. And you spend every wakin' second fixin' up her steering assembly. You'll get the word as soon as she can be turned midflight. Savvy?" She extended her palm to him. "Pardners?"

His hand was shaking with excitement as he extended it and he instantly steadied himself. "All right," he said in a controlled voice.

She threw off the last dreg in the glass and got up. Before she opened the door she gave him a broad wink. "You're a good boy, Mr. Corday. I know we're in good hands."

CHAPTER 5

The bridge was midships, deck running the total diameter and perpendicular, like all decks, to the line of march. Like a belt around her center ran the observation ports, and jutting a trifle from her otherwise smooth lines were the bridge wings, bubbles of gamma- and psi-proof glass from which a landing could be conned. The metal controls were dull beneath a coating of scum and the meter faces and screens were smudged with fingerprints. Half the dials were broken and the deck coating was worn through to the metal in the most frequented places. But it was a bridge and there was something of silence and smartness there.

Every five ship-hours the watch changed, the captain relieved by Hale, Hale relieved by Corday, Corday relieved by the captain. But it was a strange procession of reliefs. For Jocelyn stood his watch in his cabin with a stand-in on the bridge and Corday was accompanied on the bridge by a junior watch officer who should have been called a guard, since he knew nothing of the mechanics of control.

The captain's stand-in was the ship's atmosphere pilot, a man whose name had degenerated to Swifty, a satire on the fifteen hundred miles an hour his scout plane could do. E*n voyage*, his charger, was housed in its hangar aft, and as one of the engine force was assigned to its maintenance as additional duty, the atmosphere pilot could be pressed into service here.

Swifty was young, English, and always staggering drunk. He had come out of a war now three centuries forgotten to find that peace was dull and women were fickle. He had signed on the long passage of his own free will and he took his pay in whiskey. And while he could not have conned a landing of such a large vessel, he could be trusted—captain within call—on a routine watch. Pink-cheeked and blear-eyed he would stagger up a companionway from officers' country, plant a full bottle ceremoniously on the ledge before the communicator, give a low salaam to Corday and flop into a seat in the wing. Corday was then to consider himself relieved.

Alan would make his log entry, give a last hating glance at the outer dark and plunge below to busy himself with steering assemblies. For five hours he would slave over the plans, tracing leads and fuel tanks. Then, for a restless and worried four and a half hours, he would sleep. And then, gulping down a soggy breakfast in the wardroom, he would plunge up the companionway to the bridge to find Hale wearily looking for him.

Hale was important. He did all the navigation and he had a lot to teach which Corday had to know. He had been very amazed at first to find the second so transformed but with gruff heartiness set about instruction. It meant a little from Corday's sleep and a little from Hale's relief. But each change, it got a half-hour's instruction across which Corday could then pore over and digest in the remainder of his watch.

It took some of his supreme confidence away about his own education, this navigation. For Hale was proudly a "practical man" which meant simply that he hadn't been to school. The big, blustery spaceman had learned his mathematics so long ago that Corday could barely follow them. Just as he had difficulty understanding the archaic speech of the people aboard, he had infinite trouble deciphering the tattered texts by which Hale swore.

Algernon Leckwalader's "First Steps" was Corday's worst hurdle. Leckwalader thrived on obtuseness and told anecdotes. He began with a page full of "ifs" and would not commit himself beyond an occasional "probably." He favored spectrum navigation and the three-dimensional plot which he derived from descriptive geometry.

"When I first took up the business of bein' a space artist," Hale had said, "I figured you just made up your mind where you was goin' and went. But there's a lot of dead ships full of deader men out here that found it don't work. If you don't mean to become a derelict in orbit around some furrin' star, you better digest all you can get your paws on. Every time we get back we hope to find some other bucket of bolts with later pilots than us. They don't print them on Earth, you see, aside from a little hand-copied stuff they want fifty, hundred thousand dollars for around the spaceports. So that leaves a man with his own ship's logs and observations. And stars change.

"Now behind you, you see stuff one way and ahead you see it another. Age is strung out to the rear and run up a few hundred dozen times to the front. Wouldn't be so bad if you was always goin' or comin' from the same stars. But you ain't. So you have to calculate the spectrum for each angle of approach and departure and the spectrum changes for every angle. So it's a pile of memory. But we navigate in close so you only have to know about a thousand spectrums for each of sixteen navigational stars and then you got identity."

"But how do you know Earth?" Corday had consistently asked.

"Well, Earth's easy. You just figure out where it ain't and head for where you guess it may be and pick out a pinpoint amongst a lot of bigger pinpoints and you come right on in. You read Leckwalader on Star Selection, Mr. Corday."

And so it would go, confused and uncertain. But watch after watch, and in the spare hours of his duty day, Corday studied. He got so he could hold a celestolabe steady and get a fair sight and finally progressed to a point where he knew what he was getting a sight on.

And Queen, now and then, would pass with a wink

and a nudge and ask after the steering jets and balances in a cigar-husky voice.

It was this assembly which gave him the most worry. He was at a point where he dreamed tube systems. The *Hound*'s jets had been rebuilt three more times than the Deuce had known. And after many a painful tussle, crawling in cramped compartments, a conference with the diminutive chief would disclose new difficulties.

The system was essentially simple. Thirty jets in a ring around the nose, thirty in a ring around the tail. The old *Hound* had been built a man-o'-war and she had been made to maneuver. But later men had had other ideas for her, ideas which had never been written down. Apparently she had but sixteen jets now working. Originally all jets had operated from two fuel tanks, but these had been preempted for water storage when they refitted her for the long passage and new leads had been installed from the chemical landing fuel tanks. But such an arrangement is dangerous as a fission landing is always possible but fission steering is not, due to the intermittency of the required blasts and the minor caliber of force needed. And some genius had hidden two new steering tanks, one in the bow, one in the stern, and had cut in only eight of the thirty, bow and stern. Which eight fired was a matter of outside inspection, icebox stuff.

Corday did it with magnetic shoes clinging to the hull and absolute zero pressing his spacesuit a fraction of an inch from his body. He found the tubes and marked them and returned, chilled despite his heating unit, chilled enough to shiver for twenty hours after in the not-too-warm ship.

Feverishly he reconnected leads, refitted pumps, reinforced feeds and generally got on with the business. But he was irked by the petty duties with which Jocelyn distracted him.

"Mr. Corday," Jocelyn would say, as Alan came down from his watch, "decks fifteen and twenty are hog pens. Take ten men and a petty officer and see personally that they get cleaned. How can you let your people live in such filth?" And Alan would rage behind an obedient face and do as he was told.

Or, "Mr. Corday, we've another communicator breakdown between bow and second con."

Or, "Mr. Corday, take three men and check the spoiled stores. That confounded cook will have us all down with bellyaches."

And Jocelyn would hold him in idle conversation

about recent books and music or ask him about some recent discovery in engineering and would burn an hour or two of irreplaceable time. Alan felt the man sensed his second's impatience to be off and liked to annoy him with these idle time wasters.

Three times he felt he would have the steering system ready in the next watch. Three times he suffered disappointment on discovery of a bad fitting or a broken pump.

"I admire the way you're buckling down, Mr. Corday," Jocelyn told him one day. "A few more weeks like this and you'll make a first-rate officer."

Alan was suspicious of sarcasm but it was one of those rare moments when cynicism and contempt did not mar Jocelyn's splendid face. Then Corday felt guilty and crawled off to his bunk to wonder how low a man of honor can fall.

CHAPTER 6

Too much work, too little sleep and bad air mixed a combination too strong at last for Alan Corday. At this stage of his career, whatever legends say to the contrary, he was only a very young man and a young man without experience to steady him and without a solid backlog of reversals to teach him his capacities. He had been living feverishly on hope for days beyond his counting and the high flame of expectancy burned fast on the fuel of his strength.

He was not certain just when it was he began to fail. One watch he was quivering with the excitement of having learned at last how to locate Sun. The next he discovered himself staring apathetically at his calculation board, barely able to hear Hale's amiable rumble a foot from his ear.

"I said, 'Now plot Vega,'" repeated Hale.

"I beg pardon?"

"Say, what's the matter with you? I been beating my lungs out putting know-how into you and you been dreamin' about the lost plate fleet. Hello, Skipper."

"Something the matter with our young friend?" asked Jocelyn.

Hale leaned far over the plotting board and looked back into Alan's face. After a very critical inspection he shrugged. "Well, call it space fever. 'Tain't the gravity jigs nor yet the air weebles."

"I think Mr. Corday needs a rest," said Jocelyn.

"No, no!" said Alan. "No, I'm all right."

"Mr. Corday," said Jocelyn, "they are having a singsong in the crew's mess hall. I told them I would come. Go down in my stead. I'll take your watch."

"No! I'm all right!"

"Permit me to observe," said Jocelyn, "that you have just received an order."

Alan got up and found his legs unsteady under him. The bridge seemed to swim and he righted it with difficulty. The band of black ports all around it started to revolve. He stopped them.

"Yes, sir," he said, and fumbled for the companionway. His guard, Gow-eater, followed him, laughing with pleasure at this shift of duty. It was not that Gow-eater ever stopped his nervous cackling but it took on different notes and this was one of pleasure. The man lived for his bunk and his pipe, and his pay went extravagantly to Marby the ship's steward for small black pills adulterated half a hundred times. He was the most reliable man aboard when it came to a simple duty—a threat to take away opium would even stop his chuckling. Of him Jocelyn had said, "I'll trust a man with loyalty, even if it's only to a small black pill." Gow-eater couldn't sing but he liked singing and he was impatient as he had to help his charge along.

The strum of stringed instruments hummed up the ladder into the mess hall and Alan felt his way down to the strains of "Spacemen Never Die."

The music stopped as he entered and half a hundred faces, women and men, turned to him expectantly. He came out of his daze long enough to realize that he was Jocelyn's representative and said:

"Captain's compliments. Regrets absence. Be pleased to attend in his stead." And he sank thankfully into the chair they'd reserved for Jocelyn. What was the matter with him suddenly? He tried to locate Queen in the crowd and give her a reassuring nod, but she was busy pouring beer and fighting off the maudlin advances of a driveman. Alan sank back.

The orchestra, a small, off-key collection of strings and one horn, struck up, with the license of such occasions, "The Captain's Alibi." The beer passed around, voices bellowed the choruses and feet stamped. Alan sat leadenly and dull, fighting off what looked like lowering curtains of darkness.

"Go on and sing," said somebody beside him. And he saw that Mistress Luck was there, pressing a beer mug at him. "It isn't much but it's all we've got, honey. A few songs, a few kisses— Go on and sing."

He tried to manage a chorus but he didn't know it and realized suddenly that he was barely whispering anyway. A crewman handed him a glass of flaming spirits and he downed it with the hope that he would come around. He did for a little while. And then they gave him another and yet another.

He was very hazy afterwards as to what happened. He awoke once to find himself looking at a ring of young faces drawn off from the crowd to which he was teaching a ditty he had learned in school against the competition of the orchestra. And he awoke again to find the arm of Mistress Luck about him and her breath cool against his hot cheek. He could afterwards vividly recall a ragged tenor singing "The Castaway Song" and a girl with a husky, wanton voice half whispering "Heart For Sale." But his first recollection that he could identify as his own came after. How long after he did not know.

The little girl with the dirty face was stirring up some broth beside his bunk. Snoozer, the captain's runner, with a fresh bruise on her cheek.

"Hello," he said weakly.

Her eyes flashed wide in fright and she backed up from him, and then she recovered herself and came closer with the broth.

"Drink it," she said.

But he had drifted away.

When he next knew anything she was still there, but the bruise was gone and her hand was bandaged instead. She was sitting, half asleep, when he first opened his eyes but she came up like a ramrod as he moved his head.

"Please don't rave anymore," she said. And she hurriedly began to stir some powdered milk into a water glass.

The words turned Alan cold. "Who's been in here?"

"The doctor."

That was bad enough. "Anyone else?"

"The . . . the captain twice."

"Quick! What did I say?" for the chill fear of it was on him.

"Nothing! Please don't shout at me. Please don't!" And she began to cry.

He lay back and took the milk. "You are sure I said nothing? Neither to the captain nor to Strange?"

"I . . . I don't know about the doctor," she said, scrubbing at her eyes and smearing the grime. "He came many times."

"*Many* times!" said Alan. "How long have I been here?"

"I don't count watches anymore," she said. "It's been a long time."

"Has . . . has Queen been here?"

She tightened her small jaw. "She came up, but I wouldn't let her in. I couldn't stop the captain, could I, and you . . . you might have died if I'd stopped the doctor." And she began to cry.

Alan writhed like a criminal at her tears. He put aside his worry about Strange. He would see the man soon enough, he knew. That he had not been shot out of hand seemed to demonstrate that Jocelyn did not know. He fumbled out with his hand, rather amazed to see how thin and shaky it was and amazed again to feel how thin was her arm.

"Come here." He drew her over gently to the side of his bed. "Who assigned you to this job?"

She straightened up, all valiance. "Nobody. Do I have to be told to do everything?"

He looked at her oddly. "Why did you do it?"

"Because I could. Tito has my runner's job when I'm gone now. Because—" She averted her face and got very busy with another glass of powdered milk. "Because maybe I couldn't make myself not do it. Drink this."

Alan fumblingly took the milk. He regarded her with a dawning appreciation. Drowsiness was coming over him, a healthy drowsiness. "You know," he smiled, "I saw a painting like you once . . . the painting of a countess. . . . If you'd wash your face you'd . . . you'd—"

The girl caught the glass before it spilled and set it on the table. She put his unresisting arm under the covers and pulled the blanket to his chin and then stood back, looking at him with her head cocked first on one side and then the other, a proud smile on her face. Then, exhausted, she curled up with the comfort of never having known anything else on the hard metal deck and was soon asleep.

The next thing Alan knew, he was awake and alone and Dr. Strange was standing close beside him, ruddy face limned with his deceptively holy gray whiskers. The girl was gone and the door was shut.

Dr. Strange was smiling an odd smile.

"Well, how is our mutineer today?" he said.

CHAPTER 7

He wanted the log when he got around at last. He stood by Swifty for half an hour waiting for Jocelyn to take his usual "noon" glance at the dials.

Jocelyn finally came, bored and cynical, in starched white shirt and pants and a spaceman's fatigue cap. He swept a languid, uninterested eye over the bridge.

"Hello, Mr. Corday," he said, glancing now at the meters and screens. "I see that somehow you managed to survive."

"I feel very well now, sir," said Alan.

Jocelyn squared around and looked straight at him. His inspection was brief but he saw what he wanted. "You can always tell the strong ones," he said. "They don't crawl to bed at the first sneeze." And he went on with the dials.

Knifed by the injustice, Alan started to hurl a hot reply but he quickly recollected his purpose here. He wanted a look at the log. He had to know how many watches had passed, what average speed had been made and, in short, he wanted to be able to compute how much Earth time had been let go.

"If I could be entered in the log as returned to duty, I would be much obliged, sir."

Jocelyn said nothing. He was checking Hale's navigation now, left there when Hale went off watch but locked down for only the captain's key.

"If I could be entered in the log—"

"You need not repeat yourself, Mr. Corday," said Jocelyn, closing the navigation workbook with a snap and locking it. "My hearing is extremely good." He wrote a set of steering corrections on the slate above the controls, glanced at the steersman to see if he was awake and looked back at Alan. A very faint smile was on Jocelyn's mouth. He looked on by to Swifty.

"Sir, Mr. Corday seems quite anxious about the log. He is not to be given access to it. A plain sheet of paper will take his entry as watch officer and the navigator will copy it in later. Pass the word along to the quartermasters." He looked back at Alan. "And so our poor, sick boy returns to duty."

He went down the short ladder which dropped to

his quarters and turned at the bottom. "If you ever manage to conquer some of your weaknesses, Mr. Corday, you will be instated as third in command. Until then, to you as to the crew, both the log and position book will remain secured. I call your attention to the destruction locks on both." He entered his cabin and was gone.

Alan felt weak and not just from his illness now. A pandemonium of unanswered questions racked him. He was so entirely confused that he almost blurted some of them aloud to Swifty.

But everything was the same to Swifty. It always was. He had poured himself a stiff jolt from his bottle, a ceremony after every dial inspection, and was now nursing it down, reading the new courses the while.

Startled and plainly scared, Alan stumbled down the companionway to the mess hall. None spoke to him, not an unusual thing for Alan but today potent with meaning.

He fumbled at the berthing doors and went distractedly down to the sick bay.

Strange was there at the far end, feet on his white desk, spectacles unused on his forehead, wetting his thumb against turning the next page of the new treatise he was reading.

Unexpectedly a small form barred Alan's way. Still wrapped in his dirty floor-length man's jacket and with the identical dirt on his face, the "assistant surgeon"— as the crew joshed him—blocked off the far end of the sick bay.

"The doctor is very busy," said the child.

"See here," began Alan.

"He gave very big orders that he was not to be disturbed. Not by you, Mr. Corday, especially."

Alan would have brushed the child aside. But the doctor, although it would have been impossible for him to have missed this conversation held so near him, gave no sign.

Irresolute, Alan took a step forward. Placidly the doctor turned his page, raised his spectacles a little higher on his forehead and went on reading.

Breathing hard now, Alan suddenly thrust the child aside and strode forward. He slapped the book down to the desk. The doctor's spectacles dropped with a click to the bridge of his nose and he looked up with mild surprise.

"Why, Mr. Corday."

"See here, I am certain you've told. You said you

would not. You cheat! I promised you my pay for the entire cruise—"

"Mr. Corday, if you were stood against a bulkhead and shot, which is the lot of a mutineer as anyone on this ship can attest, you would draw no pay. The information is worth about fifteen thousand dollars to me if I keep it to myself. I am very good at keeping things to myself, Mr. Corday. Now if you will just close the door quietly as you leave—"

"But he knows!" said Alan. "I am sure that he does!"

"And what convinces you?"

"He . . . he—" but now the evidence did not look so good. "He barred me from the log and the navigation book."

"Captain Jocelyn," chuckled Strange, "is a man of uncertain moods and extravagant whims. Perhaps he does know. Of that you may or may not have a future clue. But you will recall a day, shortly after you came aboard, here in this hospital?"

Alan did recall it. The spaceman had fallen not three feet from where he now stood.

"You're still alive, Mr. Corday. And so I doubt that our gallant captain has just the evidence you suspect.

But he might, he might. A deep man, Mr. Corday. A very deep man." And he propped his glasses upon his forehead, readjusted his feet on the desk and located his place in *Abnormal Psychology*, Volume III, "Methods Used by the Asian Secret Police To Create Insanity." Placidly he became once more absorbed in his book.

Alan shivered. He stepped back, gingerly avoiding the place where the spaceman had fallen, and left the sick bay. Behind him, just as he closed the door, he thought he heard the doctor laugh. But he could not be sure.

Minutes ahead of time, drawn white with his recent illness and present uncertainty, Alan relieved Hale. Here he thought he might have a clue. Hale ran brook deep; every emotion of the man played on his face like searchlights from within.

But Hale was drowsy, yawning, leaning half over the drive communicator, and he gave Alan as little attention as though he had been a steersman.

"Keep her at least two thousand miles short of Constant," he said, stifling a yawn. "The Deuce has got hot atoms back there all of a sudden. She came up within a thousand half an hour ago and I check-blasted back. I'm bored."

"Then I relieve you, sir," said Alan.

"But we'll be at Johnny's Landing in about thirty watches. Then watch me kick my heels." The thought cheered him and he laughed. "They got a concoction there they call 'low fission' but there's nothing low about its effects. Tobacco juice, red pepper, HCL and a dash of strychnine—the last to keep the heart goin'. Here's a blank sheet for your entry." And he was gone below.

Alan had strained to catch every nuance of Hale's rumble. Surely the man was incapable of playing a part. He had always thought so. But now he wasn't quite as sure. The blank sheet Hale had flung to him had chilled the effect of the friendlier utterances.

And then the light beam which shined in the distant nose of the *Hound* began to catch too many of its own particles back in its face too fast and the speed dial crept up to one hundred and eighty-four thousand five hundred. Alan spoke sharply to the communicator man:

"Check blast five hundred."

"Check blast five hundred, sir." And then, "Drives receipt check blast five hundred, sir."

Bridge discipline had relaxed when Hale went aft. "She smells a bone at Johnny's Landing," said the steersman to a quartermaster.

"Just so you aren't on trick to crash us in and plow it up," was the petty officer's brittle retort.

"Silence on the bridge," said Alan.

They looked at him without respect and complied for a while.

Alan felt the deck grow a trifle heavier under him and glanced at the speed dial. She was riding now at one hundred and eighty-four one hundred.

"Check blast one hundred."

"Check blast one hundred," acknowledged the communicator man, omitting the "sir" as a rebuke for the silence command. "Drives receipt check blast one hundred."

Alan kept his eyes on the speed dial. It sagged back to one hundred and eighty-three nine hundred and hung there. It annoyed him. And he was about to give the engineer watch a warning bell to get on its toes when suddenly the littleness of his authority, the insecurity of his position, his uncertainty and his thwarted hopes all settled over him, a cloud on top of his convalescence.

Dispiritedly he threw in a gong which would be tripped if one hundred and eighty-five thousand miles per second would be reached and took himself off to the bridge wing.

The stars were cold and inhospitable before, behind, above, below. The scarred hull of the *Hound* gleamed faintly with the particle absorption of fast flight. He could feel the chill of absolute zero even through the ray-proof panes. Dark and cold, cold with a cold wherein no motion was possible in fluid or gas.

He put his arm against the rail and buried his face in his jacket sleeve to shut it out and so he stayed through half his watch. The gong rang three times and then three times again.

Let her go. Let her edge on up to Constant. Let her flash on through zero time and explode to pure energy or let her hang as one ship had at the exact speed of light and hang there forever, impervious, unmoving, her people statues within her, locked, protected and condemned to eternity by zero time.

Jocelyn's voice was thin with contempt. "Am I disturbing your rest, Mr. Corday? Or are you sitting this one out? Quartermaster, check blast a thousand."

Startled, Alan stared into the bridge. Only the communicator man, the steersman, the quartermaster, were there. The bridge speaker had opened and it clicked shut now.

Stammering, Alan repeated, "Check blast one thousand!"

The communicator man did not answer him. The needle on his dial stood already at that figure. He brought the handles back and the gong stopped ringing.

Alan waited the remaining two and one-half hours for Jocelyn to come to the bridge. But Jocelyn did not come.

The gong had not been loud enough to reach to Jocelyn's soundproof quarters. He had not known the captain had a repeated dial. But Jocelyn did not come and Alan kept the speed as near one hundred and eighty-four as human error and the grossness of drives would permit.

Swifty came up, put his bottle down on the

communicator ledge, scanned the dials, scratched himself awake and gangled over to Alan.

"One hundred and eighty-four and steady as she goes," said Alan and hastily fled from the bridge.

There was a box of antisleep capsules on his desk. He gave them a hypnotic stare and fell exhausted on his bunk. But he did not sleep. At every footstep in the passageway he tensed; when any careless passing elbow brushed his lock he saw again the spaceman trying to get free.

And when he had at last dropped into a fitful doze a hand shook him rudely and he was sure of his fate at last.

It was only a quartermaster. "Time for your watch, Mr. Corday."

CHAPTER 8

W ell, it's like this," said Gow-eater, flopping against the rail beside Alan and waving a hand out of the port at the tangled valleys and mountains below, "if they stayed put, there wouldn't be no variety in it."

They were in second con, standing by preparatory to landing. It was an all-hands evolution and, the ship being about a quarter manned, everyone down to five years of age had his or her post. It took a lot to bring the *Flea Circus* to ground, particularly where no landing racks had been provided, and in strange areas Jocelyn liked to have at least token crews on her after-batteries just in case somebody proved hostile.

They had been bobbing now for about ten hours above the planet Johnny's Landing, waiting for Swifty to come back in his dilapidated atmosphere craft and tell them where the population had got to.

Gow-eater had been without his "black fuel" for

many watches, but anticipating a new supply, he had mellowed himself pleasantly. "I ain't no hand at guessin' at time, but I swear it couldn't be more than five hundred planet-years since we hit this place. There was a row of buildings right down there where you see that river turning between the green cliffs. They was strung out along the top with the fields behind. Some mighty pretty girls, mighty pretty. And obligin', too. New planted place, mebbe a thousand years old by now, though it's easy to get mixed. Been a ship-year since we was here and my memory's bad anyhow. Course, might be twelve hundred planet-years since we hit the place—I might have mislaid a trip. But no, I think it's nearer five hundred.

"Nice place. Diamonds in that river gravel big as biscuits—uranium in that string of hills over there so's a counter nigh kills itself—and they raise mighty good apples. You sure you don't even see a foundation left, Mr. Corday?"

Alan obligingly looked for the tenth time since planet dawn and then laid his glasses aside. "Nothing on those bluffs but grass."

"Well, Swifty'll find 'em. He's the dangedest gent for findin' things. Especially girls. But don't recall his takin' ten hours before on anything." Gow-eater began to fidget. "You don't suppose he found 'em and landed for his own good time, do you? The skipper'd kill him!"

A gong clanged and they stood more precisely to their stations. The ten-year-old kid who was handling second con's communicator bent a keen, veteran eye out the port and said, "There comes the—"

"Bill," said his mother sharply from her post at the phones, "you watch your language."

"Well, he does anyhow," said the undaunted Bill.

They watched their controls moving in repeat to main con, for this was only the emergency bridge, manned against machinery jams or shellfire. It was close to the drives, and the chemical explosions as the big vessel edged ahead made the auxiliary bridge rumble and the compasses slide back and forth on the chart board. The finite dial climbed sluggishly to six hundred mph.

There was a dull thump and a whine of machinery as the atmosphere plane was drawn into the hull.

The woman on the phones waited as long as her curiosity could stand it and then said, "Irma! I mean bridge. What's he say?"

The people at secondary looked alertly at the

phone station and the woman tipped them a head bob which meant she was getting it, to be patient.

The controls moved spectrally under the second quartermaster's gaze and the *Hound of Heaven* edged to planet northeast and picked up speed. They ran rapidly to dusk and then altered course, turning due north to parallel a silver lake of great length which shortly became a river.

"Irma says there's a vessel up here. Swifty changed signals with it and he thinks it's the *King's Lion* out of Boston. He took so long to tell the whole of it because he was so dry." She laughed fondly and then straightened her face quickly. "Don't you ever take to drink," she snapped at Bill.

"Honest to Pete," said Bill in shrill exasperation, "I—"

"Shut up," said his mother. "He says there's a town up by the seacoast. Was there a sea on this planet, Gow-eater? No, that was Idylwild that didn't have a sea over on the Mizar beat."

"I didn't have no time to look at seas," said Gow-eater with a grin. "But they better be as industrious as we left 'em."

"Trade prices will be bad," said the woman. "Confounded Boston ship."

"Don't crab about it," said Gow-eater. "That's the first hooker in our own class that we've struck out here in two ship-years."

"There she is!" said Bill, off station again.

A moment later bridge sighted her with the help of metonic locators and the uneasy situation of second con in regard to gravity—since her decks were perpendicular to planet surface in this cruising position—was corrected by the bow pointing skyward as they crawfished down.

Twenty minutes later they were sitting on their tail beside a thundering sea which glowed in the deepening darkness and the crews of each vessel were mingling on the intervening sand.

Alan stood by himself, glad to feel ground, glad to breathe clean air, not quite as nervous as he was, since time spent here was equal with Earth time, but anxious to be away all the same.

From the scraps of conversation in the groups around him, he gathered that while the two vessels had known of each other they had never before met.

He listened awhile to two long-passage men trying to find common ground and shuddered. They had been born in the same town, Old Angeles; they were more or less of age, about forty. But the family of the *Lion* spaceman had been scattered and forgotten two hundred years before the *Hound* spaceman had been born. And they considered it a coincidence that they should be "so close of a time." They swapped tobacco, groped for some common conversational ground, played out Old Angeles in a very few words and fell silent. Then one of them hopefully brought up the agreeableness of the women on Caterdice of Deneb and this promptly lapsed when the other expressed surprise, since during the age of his visit the dominant race there had been African pygmy labor importation. They came at last to the solid ground of optimum chemical fuel mixtures and sat down with great relief to a pleasant talk.

Alan wandered off, feeling lonely and shunned. He looked up at the darkening sky where a few last rays of the setting star painted the tall clouds green and gold, and so different was the aspect of that sight from Earth that he realized suddenly, dishearteningly, where he was, how incalculably far he was from home.

A voice reached him from near at hand, dimmed by the surf but carried on the thin breeze of evening. It was dark enough along the beach now to see cigarettes glowing in the various groups and he stood quite near the captain of the *Lion* and Jocelyn without being seen.

Jocelyn was sitting on driftwood, limned against the glow of the bursting surf, snapping pebbles at the charging waves.

"You're sure you've searched thoroughly," he was saying.

"Tucked up and left, far's I can see, Cap'n. Bread in the oven, plows in the field, pigs and chickens gone wild all through the bresh. I kem in ter fix me up a trade on some of that air yewranium last planet-week."

"This wouldn't be a dodge to get me to sheer off, would it, Captain?"

"Jocelyn, though I be from Boston I wouldn't make any man burn atoms in such a wasteful fashion, not if he war my most blessit enemy."

Jocelyn pitched another pebble. "How about the mines?"

"You ain't thinkin' of minin'!"

"I was thinking of raids," said Jocelyn. "Mines all right, no raid."

"Well, they're all right ca'se I took a meander up thar. But six blessit days lookin' by my airyplane ain't disclosed whatever. They tucked up and left."

"I was here a ship-year ago but I compute that here at six hundred planet-years. Swifty!"

"Aye, aye!" from a crowd of *Lion* girls and shortly a lurching Swifty.

"Swifty," said Jocelyn, "we've got a mystery here. You get a stretch of beach clear and clip off. Take that Bill Godine and look until you find a colony."

"Aye, aye, Skipper. Shucks, another one empty. Hey, young Bill!"

The ten-year-old skipped away from his mother, eyes big and bright.

"Young Bill," said Swifty, "you are about to take your jolly old life in your two bare hands. Hip, hip. Tell Jock to tower away and all that. Hello, Corday. Would you get some people to clear that bally driftwood off the silver strand?"

The Deuce threw some power behind the searchlights and the stub-winged jet, ten minutes later, flamed up into the black sky and was gone.

Alan found himself wandering with groups toward the town, along a road overgrown with grass, between walls fallen into round, lichen-covered piles.

But he couldn't take very much of the town. Where

the roofs were still intact one could enter houses and find there strewn toys, set tables, and what the sea air had left of clothing not worn these fifty years. The wandering groups of spacemen and women touched nothing, not from honesty but from a highly developed sense of luck. But soon their superstition faded away enough to bring about the election of a mayor, the making of a bonfire from tattered park benches and the trial and execution of a wild pig which was promptly cooked and eaten. Somebody else discovered a cellar and Alan at length found himself on the outskirts of a singing crew, forgetful already with bumpers of sweet wine.

The cold dawn found Jocelyn and an exhausted Swifty hard at work rousing the crews of both ships from various postures of abandon, and during the whole planet-day there was not one man or woman aboard the *Lion* or the *Hound* who did not groan and shudder at the mention of sweet wine.

They transferred their landing to the site of the mines and spacemen, with many a curse and protest and many an alarmed eye on Geiger counters, turned miners.

Ten days later, payloaded to the safety limit and

the whole vessel smelling of dirt, they shoved ground for Earth while the *Lion*, with another market in mind, headed out towards Pollux.

Of the colony's fate they had no faintest clue.

"Note it down in your Star Pilot, Mr. Hale," said Jocelyn. "Johnny's Landing is open for a colony. A colony with some brains."

CHAPTER 9

Hope beat high in the breast of Alan Corday as the watches went round. Inconsistently he found himself, whenever he was on watch, willing the speed dial higher. That in itself was madness but the coldly logical part of him was not yet highly developed and home is an emotional thing.

He was going *home*. He had no idea of his distance from Earth, the number of ship-hours which had elapsed or the number of years which had passed on Earth. But he was young and with each passing watch the hope beat higher. Perhaps less than fifteen years would have passed. If that were true, then he could realize his goals.

Now there was no idea of holding back from duty. He was swift to obey commands, meticulous in the performance of duty, scornful of Gow-eater's lurking presence. While he was very far from the best watch officer that could be made, he began to bring enthusiasm into his job and he was easily the best, next to Jocelyn, aboard. He studied, not navigation, but ship repair and control. He conceived all manner of possible incidents or accidents which might slow them and he set himself to thoroughly know how to best meet each one.

Whatever his former moods, none could complain of him now. In days, by a steady application of an actually brilliant mind, he digested all the emergency drills of the big ship, mastered damage control and perfected his own ship handling. He was sharp with Hale about curved space computation and in this Hale was apt to be slack, running wide from carelessness and correcting. Hale, surprised, humored him and even tightened up with an amiable guffaw. Every minute of ship time saved on this run meant days of saved Earth time to Corday.

He was cheerful and alert and even the bridge crew, despite the suspicion of a very insular life aboard, warmed to him enough to say "sir." Queen he passed with complete amnesia about such things as mutiny. The Deuce he used to get a little more precision out of check blasting. Jocelyn he suffered as a necessary evil, adopting the happy attitude that whatever the man was, he was getting Alan home.

Corday began to laugh easily and naturally over minor discomforts. In a superior way he began to be very tolerant of the dirt caused by a spaceship's perpetual shortage of water, of the antique speech of the crew and the odd morals of her officers. He could afford tolerance. He was going *home*.

Sometimes, when his cabin was dark and the ship skin cold with the absolute zero outside, actuality and doubt would try to struggle to the surface of his mind. But he thrust them down. He was young. He had hope. He had a *home*.

Only three other men aboard had any interest in the matter, another point of superiority Alan held over the ship's complement. They were outcasts. They belonged nowhere. Their time had lagged until they had no hope anywhere. But he was different. Three of the kidnaped spacemen who had boarded, perforce, with him, were anxious to get back. The other eleven were apathetic, having reasons of their own not to love Earth. But with the three, Corday found himself in frequent conversation about the joys of Earth.

They forgot top-heavy and turbulent governments;

they forgot how hot Newer York could be. They forgot racial squabbles and economic affairs. All Earth was a paradise in which no faults dwelt that could not be forgotten or forgiven.

Now and then, on watch, studying with Hale or wandering along on some routine job which required little thought, the time equations would rouse to haunt him. They were such precisely accurate things. There was no compromise with Einstein nor with Lorentz.

$$M_v = \frac{M_o}{\sqrt{1 - \dfrac{V^2}{C^2}}}$$

$$T_v = T_o \cdot \sqrt{1 - \frac{V^2}{C^2}}$$

And now and then he would write them idly on a pad, discover what he was doing, look aghast at their value for velocity—seldom less than one hundred eighty-four thousand miles per second, usually more—and with horror rub them out.

He was blinding himself purposely and he half

realized it more than once when he made mistakes in the inbound watch number he set down on his separate log sheet. What he did not realize was that he would carry the same watch number for four or more consecutive log entries, willfully deluding himself completely as to the number of ship-weeks it was taking homeward bound.

If there was any note of hysteria in his enthusiasm for getting the ship along, he was the last to sense it. He had a cocky swagger about the whole thing, a swagger which yet would not permit his complete calculation of the years which had fled on Earth.

He joined in the singing and he played acey-trays with Hale. He made high-flown plans and was cunning to prepare their carrying out. With desperate psychology he engaged Strange in many a bitter battle over a chessboard in sick bay and by whipping at the doctor's vanity with such remarks as "You know, it's a funny thing about chess—a man feels the disgrace of a beating so keenly, I think, because there's no luck in it—getting mated is a truthful commentary on a man's actual brains—" before half the voyage was done he had won back his entire pay and three thousand besides. With his share of the uranium cargo—and he had turned suddenly deaf to a chilling remark of Marby's: "Hope Earth is still using the stuff when we get there. Recall what happened two trips back with that gold?"—Alan would have nearly twenty-five thousand dollars when he was paid off.

And he pushed the speed dial and denied that the faster they went, the more Earth time they burned. And he falsified his log to himself. And he felt he was thrusting the *Flea Circus* home with his own push alone. It was almost a happy time for him. Chica would not have changed, New Chicago would be simply New Chicago. And what a lark he'd have telling his onetime classmates about the tremendous adventure he'd had in the stars. Make good table conversation— casual reference to a lost colony—odds and ends like, "Aboard those ships you can never tell who you're rubbing elbows with. Why on the *King's Lion*—built two thousand years ago, by the way, in some place called Boston—there was a murderer who—" And Chica would beam and bring on the port and his friends would urge him to say more—

"Mr. Corday," said Jocelyn coldly, "if you can spare a moment from your daydreaming, you can rig the starboard gangway. Needs two new sheaves and a brace. We'll be decelerating steadily now so don't spill a man off the side."

"You mean we're almost in?"

"Ten watches, Mr. Corday. Our heaters have been running on Sun particles for two ship-days. Or have you been elsewhere?"

And then, swimming up at them, green and blue and shimmering, was the loveliest sight in the heavens—Earth! She came to them like a grand queen, robed in her silvery mists, attended by her page, the Moon. And the Sun corona flamed beyond her in a fireworks of welcome.

Alan, quivering with impatience, nostrils flared with the emotions which roared in him, writhed at the senseless precautions of "this fool Jocelyn." For, on coming into atmosphere, off went Swifty with the Deuce to "take a scout and locate any possible wars or commotions, taking due care to fly well beyond the possible ranges and accuracies of any new weapons."

For five hours they stood to battle quarters, barely within the outermost atmosphere, moving in an erratic course, all detectors alert.

Senseless precautions, fumed Alan. There'd been

no scent of wars when they left and wars could be seen for twenty years ahead. And indeed, the precautions were apparently senseless, for at dusk they dropped down to the flats of New Chicago into the racks of the greatest spaceport on Earth.

"All hands muster in the mess hall to receive instructions," said the speakers through the ship.

"Cap'n's compliments," said Snoozer, smiling radiantly out of a miraculously clean face, "and would Mr. Corday report to his quarters."

Alan loved the world. He patted Snoozer on the head. "Aye, aye, Countess."

He had never been in the quarters before and he did not see them now, being only aware of some old ensigns coiled in the corner and a sense of large space—for these were the admiral's cabins, made for a service long dead.

Jocelyn did not look particularly unkind. "Sit down, Mr. Corday."

Impatiently Alan sat down. He was aware of the warm eyes of Mistress Luck who sat on the transom performing the unwifely act of cleaning Jocelyn's holster and gun.

"We have had several trials, Mr. Corday," said

Jocelyn. "In the normal course of the long passage there are many worse."

Alan nodded jerkily, anxious to be off.

"You are very young," said Jocelyn, "and you have a very great deal to learn. But with application you may possibly someday make an excellent third in command." He stretched out his legs and began to toss a small desk knife from hand to hand. "You possibly conceive your liberty to have been violated when you came with us and doubtless have many complaints of your treatment aboard. I see you still bear two small scars on your right hand. I am sorry, Mr. Corday, that such measures were necessary. There is much you do not know."

Alan twisted around in the chair, trying to be polite. He could afford politeness now.

What Jocelyn was saying was being said with an effort. But Alan did not notice that. He only saw a man whom he supposed he would never see again and had no wish to know.

"Mr. Corday, I want you to consider that your position at present pay is open until we leave. We will be here ten days more or less. We shift tomorrow, according to my port advices, to the dockyard to have new drives mounted of an advanced design. We will be in Berthing 197, about a quarter of a mile north of the new warehouses they've built. You will have no trouble finding us."

"I am sure," said Alan, "that I will not see you there. I can conceive of no possible reason why I should."

"There are worse things that could happen to a man," said Jocelyn.

"If there are, sir, I cannot conceive them either."

Jocelyn bit at his lip. He looked fixedly at Alan and then reached into a panel on the desk to draw forth a slip on which he wrote Alan's name and service. Then he pulled from a bag, newly brought aboard, a sheaf of bills and counted out fifteen thousand dollars. To this he added nine thousand, "by authority of draft from Dr. Strange and by reason of a cargo share." He pushed the bills with the discharge toward Alan. They vanished quickly into the side pocket of the tattered white jacket.

"I'd get some new clothes," said Jocelyn. "That is a tenth-class jacket according to its collar insignia. At best you may find some slight changes. I have not investigated anything beyond our safety in landing."

Alan stood up. He gave a brief, formal bow to Mistress Luck and another to Captain Jocelyn.

"You will not reconsider now?" said Jocelyn. And then suddenly, "You may not like what you find, Corday. Believe me, the first return—" He bit it off and stood up, not offering his hand. Hard bitterness came suddenly back to his handsome face. "I see you won't. Goodbye, Mr. Corday."

Alan bowed again and turned on his heel. He found Snoozer in the passageway, eyes wide, stunned. He stopped to drop a bill into her hand with a jocular "Buy yourself some soap, Countess. On me."

But as he paused he caught a glimpse of Jocelyn through the open door. The man had poured himself a stiff drink and into it he was emptying a powder. He drained it off and threw the glass to the floor where it splintered into a thousand diamonds.

Corday, barely registering the fact, turned away, patted Snoozer on the head and sped aft to the gangway where the sentry saluted. Behind him Alan thought he heard a girl sobbing. Some ship kid without shore leave, he thought. And then he was over the side.

In leaving, he noticed that his new-rigged sheaves had operated smoothly and that the gangway reached the precise distance to the ground. And then, without another glance at the ship, he hailed a hovering cab.

CHAPTER 10

The cabbie skimmed along, driving with one hand, right arm over the back of his seat and his face, most of the time sideways to his passenger, animated with interest.

"Say, bub, ain't that a Martian ship or something? Never seen her like."

Alan loved the world just now. "That's the *Hound of Heaven*."

"Never heard of her and I know most of the regular runs."

"She's back from the long passage."

The cabbie gave a start, looked back through his rear window and then put on a little more speed. "Why doesn't somebody tell a feller these things? I was right there when she landed expectin' a good all-night cruise around the fireworks dispensaries with a thirsty convoy. Whew! Glad you tipped me, bub. Them babies are man-hungry." He suddenly turned back to Alan. "Meanin' no offense, you understand. I didn't mean—"

"I'm through with her," said Alan happily. "And I know what you mean."

The cabbie was relieved. "Well, then! Don't get 'em in very often. Been two, three months since one of them buzzards was around. And the cops stood ten deep tryin' to keep her from leavin'. But no use. Wonder why somebody don't keep a docket on 'em so's they'd control themselves. But heck, a police department can't hardly stay in power long enough to catch the same ship again. Read the other day where somebody was arguin' that they was a necessary evil, bringin' in occasional wealth and providin' the dockyards with work at fancy prices. But me, I can't see it. Now a nice, quiet clambake with a Martian run crew— You ain't told me what guzzle emporium we make first, bub. You been gone long?"

"Not very," said Alan with confidence. "And I'm not heading for a fast night."

"Well, you can have one, let me tell you, so don't make up your mind too fast. Ever since we got the church out of power, old New Chi has been runnin' wide open and full-soused."

Alan nodded, preoccupied with his expectations, twenty-four thousand sweet in his pocket. And then the cabbie's remark failed to mesh properly with his thoughts. "I beg pardon?"

"Wide open!" said the cabbie. "There's Barracoon Bob's, for instance, where you get a glass of filleroo, an armful of—"

"I mean this church thing," said Alan, still determined not to take any news seriously.

"Well?"

"I mean you said since the church was knocked out of power. I didn't know there was a church *in* power."

The cabbie looked back confusedly. "Look, bub. You sure you ain't had two or six already tonight?" And then he gave a shrug. "Forgot you was off that thing back there."

"What happened?"

"Oh, the whites fixed up a church to keep down the 'common people.' That was right after the last war."

"War? What war?" said Alan, his heart beginning to sag in spite of all he could do.

"Now see here, bub, all I know is what I learned in the eighth grade. THE war, of course."

"We won?"

"Bub, did anybody ever win a war? But maybe you can say the whites won. The Beggas Guild did all the fightin' and got killed off—"

"The what?"

"That's just slang for the 'People's Party,' bub. They had a church of their own, so I been told. The Fission . . . no, the Electrician . . . shucks, some church or other. And the priests all got burned. Seen one when I was a kid. They were chasin' him down an alley and his hair was on fire. I—"

"I am very confused," said Alan. "What church won?"

"Oh, the white outfit wasn't a church, accordin' to what I been told. It was preached over the air and they used jawnotics or something like that."

"Hypnotics?"

"Well, take your choice. But whatever it was, the whites sure had people steppin' out for a while. Then Conners started a revolution and overthrew that church and made up a new one called the Christian Church. I belong."

Alan was trying to jigsaw all this together on a time track.

"Anyway, you sure missed a lot of fun. Been years

since we had any real trouble, but once in a while somebody will denounce somebody as a white and there'll be a fine hoorah and a firing party and free beer. We got a fine man in now: Justinius Murphy."

"What . . . who—?"

"Republicanites, of course. Say, you *are* a republican, aren't you? I ain't supposed to drive nobody unless he is." The driver swiveled around and looked hard. Suddenly he yanked the controls and braked. Then he turned and opened the door.

"Bub, I'm sorry. But I'm not takin' any chances. This is a free country and everybody does what he likes and all that, but I got to report it."

"See here," said Alan stiffly. "I have been gone for ten or fifteen years, true enough, but it has been a long time since a cabbie told me to get out."

"You're in the limits. And you can hoof it, bub."

Alan wondered whether he should strike the man or bribe him. He tried the latter and it failed.

"Nope. Sorry, bub. Can't take chances."

He was not used to brawling with menials and he stepped with dignity to the walk. He had some odds and ends of change as part of his pay and he extended a coin. The driver looked at it with contempt and he changed it to one four times the size which the driver accepted. It was the first time Alan noticed that he was carrying iron money with a glowing center. The bills he had barely noticed beyond their odd printing.

"Seein' you're playin' the grand duke," said the cabbie, "I'll comment that you better shuck that coat."

"Why?"

"It's white! Ain't that enough? Well, no hard feelings, bub, I . . . Judas Iscariot!" And he staggered back, pale.

Alan glanced wonderingly at his own chest. "What now?" he said, half angry.

"Look, bub. Suicide is all right in its place, but that place ain't in my vicinity. Don't walk ten feet without tearin' off that collar tab!"

"Why?"

"Why? Heavenly angels. The engineers, tenth class! I seen it in my history books, eagle, compass and all! Who do you suppose took over the world?"

Alan felt a sudden surge of sickness. Not from danger at hand. Not from any realization that his one-time comrades had once been kings—but that *time* had passed.

"History books," he repeated dully.

But the hack was gone.

An hour later, fighting still a dread prescience, striving to ignore the unfamiliar buildings which stood beside familiarly named streets, Alan came to a small park. It was a square on the second level, open all the way to sunlight in the day and stars in the night. It had not changed. The benches and the street lamps were all the same and on one of those benches— He searched quickly and from what had threatened to engulf him he gave out a short, happy laugh.

Carved with a junior-school scrawl and hardly obscured at all by paint was a heart, an arrow and two sets of initials: "A.C. lvs C.M." A silly thing, something to laugh about. They'd been young and it had been a second date and the moon had shone down through the holes in the upper squares.

"Silly kids," said Alan. He traced the initials. "Cerita Montgraine." Chica. Well, she was here someplace in the city. He knew he would find her. Maybe she was a little older than he now. Maybe she was even gray, huh? But it had been his fault and she had promised and everything was going to be all right. He'd known a fellow, Jordan Cash, in school, who had married a woman forty years old and they'd been happy as a couple of pigeons. What was age? What was age? The heart counted. And it took an older woman to properly understand a man. Who had said that? Oh, yes, Queen. Fat, globulous Queen. She was right, too.

"Sure she was right, sure she was right," said his feet in cadence as he walked down the boulevard. "Sure she was right." And he fought away the gloom. But there was something else in his bootbeats on the pavement, something he couldn't completely forget. A glib, precise thing: "Mass times Velocity," sure, the Einstein equation, "equals Mass zero divided by the square root of one minus Velocity squared divided by Constant squared enclosed." Bootbeats.

He was looking for his parents' house, his own home. His mother would be pretty old now, he knew that. And his father was probably dead, for the old fellow had been ailing ever since he had lost the firm and had had to give up the country place and his horses. But his mother at least would be living, since she came from a long-lived clan and had never been ill a day in all her enthusiastic life. He felt guilty not to have worried about her in the last many weeks. But she'd understand about a young man being in love. And she'd know where Chica was.

And then he stopped, puzzled. He went back and looked from the corner and then came on again. There was something strange about this block and yet it was most certainly the right block. There should be a garden wall— And then he sighed in deep relief. There *was* a garden wall. And he shoved at the gate and the gate gave and he stepped inside.

"Hey, what's the matter with you?"

It was a strange man, a man in a dirty shirt shoving potted plants into a box. The place was a strange sort of hothouse without any glass or lights or vats for liquid food.

"I don't sell retail and I don't pay anybody but Jimson. So get out."

"I beg pardon," said Alan. "I was looking for the Corday residence."

"The what?"

"The Sir Alton Corday residence."

"Brother, this here is a paper box factory and I rent the yard. There ain't a residence on this whole square of town. I . . . What did you say?"

"The Sir Alton—"

"I caught it. You a government man? Because if you are, there ain't any white cash buried in this place. I dug it all up when I heard about it from my old man. Not a republican! Heard there was some white plate found over on Liberty Street last year, though."

Alan looked accusingly at the garden as though it had betrayed him. Here he had braved his first rocking horse and got his first licking for pulling up the zinnias. He came back to the presence of the man. "Would . . . do you suppose anybody could tell me where the Cordays moved to?"

"Moved?" The man laughed and went back to stuffing plants in the boxes with expert economy of motion. Then he saw that Alan was still there and temporized. "You might ask next level down. The deacon that took over is an old bird and he knows the whole parish like a litany."

"I know the place well, thank you."

Alan braced up, thanked him and walked out. The gate clicked shut behind him, a small, remorseless and final click.

He felt a little dazed. Deceleration, he told himself. Being three or four gravities heavy for days made a man feel funny for a while.

The church was badly battered, shyly retired into a recess between two larger buildings. Alan noticed, when he saw its disrepair, that the whole neighborhood was out at elbows, that the streets were rutted and cratered with mud oozing through broken pavement. This had been a large church once but it had lost both wings and its steeple. Odd to see it this way when he remembered it from such a short while ago as being a noble, imposing edifice with a broad lawn and skyholes through every level all the way up. Must have been set afire recently.

It was early and his knock at the small door was quickly answered. A wizened being in a black cloak answered and bobbed his head at every word Alan spoke. But not to say yes. He continued the gesture throughout the interview and it was to signify no.

"But my family crypt is here," said Alan.

"Family? Crypt?" *Bob, bob.* "You talk like a white, young man."

"May I see the crypts?" And he gave over a coin.

"Of course, of course. And the registers too, what's left."

But a yawning hole was in the floor, and the flagstones and the names were mostly gone. Alan struck light to a votive candle and attempted to read some of the inscriptions by this flickering red glow. But although he recognized the family names of some tenth and eleventh class slabs, none bore Corday.

"Mighty puzzling," said the deacon, "just why you'd like to know," *bob, bob*, "but you're welcome to the registers—them that's left." *Bob, bob*. And he showed Alan a pile of moldy books.

But so badly were they burned along the edges that few of the pages could be read and Alan, hot wax unnoticed on his hand which held the votive light, found nothing.

"Let me see," said the deacon. "I recall a Strachay. You wouldn't want a Strachay?" And then, "Hey now. Wait. The slabs they used to repair the streets are some of 'em right side up."

Alan stared in disbelief.

"The slabs they filled the chuckhole with in front." *Bob, bob*. "Come along." And he shuffled out into the darkness.

Alan had not noticed until this moment that the first level was not only badly lighted but not lighted at all. And he had to resort to a taper for which he paid a dollar.

He was scraping away mud with his boot when he

was hailed. A man carrying a steady lantern came over and berated the deacon for "illegal sale of lights" and Alan's taper went out. He looked up to see a wolf-eyed man in rags glaring at him.

"You want light, you pay for light, my friend."

Alan was almost too distracted by his task to understand. He forced himself to answer. And he found himself cheerfully aided by a "dues-paid member of the light guild."

They scratched and mucked for half an hour with the deacon bobbing about, recommending other chuckholes and then Alan stopped suddenly. A broken slab was marked "ay."

He dug about it, heedless of the muck, trying to find another piece of it. And the light bearer heaved up whiskey-laden grunts as he pulled and the deacon bobbed about excitedly.

But that was all.

"Tell you what," said the light bearer. "I got a couple of friends up the street in the messenger way of business and we'll send for a garden digger. That's if you've got money, of course. And we'll dig up the whole blamed street." This prospect enthused him and he stood up to give the potential scene a glowing survey.

The deacon bob-bobbed that it would be a fine idea.

And then Alan saw them. He saw the mud and the ragged light bearer and the cloaked deacon and the street. He saw the church as it had been and now the church as it was.

He straightened. "Thank you," he said. "It won't be necessary. If you wish to accompany me, I will pay your hire." He turned with precision and paid the deacon who bob-bobbed thankfully. He indicated the way he would go to the light bearer.

And he turned his steps from the broken slab marked "ay."

CHAPTER 11

After walking for a long time, aimlessly, steadying himself, Alan found that they had come from under the levels and were in open country, surrounded by dilapidated shacks. He was confused as he recalled no such section, even though it was possible that during a lifetime he had not seen all of New Chicago.

"This is Brightpark," said the light bearer with the fondness of long acquaintance. "I got a place over here. Not bad. Six by six and I can near stretch out. Things have been getting better for us republicans right along. Less than thirty percent of the city is out of work and that's progress!"

"*Thirty* percent," said Alan, startled despite his glum thoughts. "I thought it was high at *ten* percent. But of course you're one of the thirty, I suppose."

"Me?" said the light bearer, insulted. "Believe me,

I'm a laborer! Yes, sir. I'm one of the seventy. How'd you think I'd get a permit to light people along? I'm industry itself, employer. And to prove it I am going to stop right here and earn a guide tip. I go, I light, you follow. That's one thing. But there's nothing in my union rules— though there's plenty in the guide rules, but what they don't know won't hurt 'em—against my pointing a couple of things out that you want to know. Where we going?"

"I have been trying to orient myself," said Alan, with considerably more truth than he knew. "This is Brightpark. I was trying to reach Brightpark. But this is not the Brightpark I know. I have made some kind of an error. Or you have. I am looking for a place that is mostly lawns, big houses and stables. Surely you must know where the racing crowd lives."

"Employer, the only racing that's done around here is cockroaches. And I can prove that by the fifty cents I lost last Monday. And this is the only Brightpark we got. You might be fussier than some, but just the same this is the Brightpark you're going to take because it's all there is."

"Granted then that the place has been . . . been subdivided. I see here to the right and left a few old homes sticking up through this rubbish. I am looking, specifically, for the Montgraine residence. Their country residence, that is, if you don't mind the old conceit of calling this country under the shadow of the levels. The home was called Sunnylawn."

"Sounds like a cemetery," said the light bearer. "Well, if you don't mind payin' a little extra for the guidin', what was the exact and precise address?"

"No address. Just Sunnylawn. The Montgraine residence. Everybody—"

"Everybody knows the place. I know. I've done guiding before this, employer. You . . . you *do* have money, don't you?"

"Of course."

"All right. There's a Montgraine Road over here about a dozen blocks. You remember what I said about extra fee."

"If it is the right place, I will double the fee," said Alan.

The light bearer promptly doubled the fee to be doubled in his own mind and led off at right angles, down through a series of broken streets and garbage-strewn alleys.

"That's my place over there," he volunteered. "The government built this whole section up about five years after the last war and they did a pretty good job, I been told. But it's kind of gone to seed now, I'll admit. This ten-by-ten lot division is a good thing, I maintain. Lets a man have a place in the good, clean open air, a house near big enough to stretch out and plenty of space left to cook in when it don't rain. There's the street."

Alan looked at the unfamiliar landscape. There were no lights, a fact which his light bearer explained was due to the need of employment for light bearers, but there was a general glow from many windows and it was possible to see contour. Sunnylawn had stood on a knoll.

"Is there a hill around here?"

"The guiding fee being in full force," said the light bearer, "there is." And he trudged off toward it.

From afar it was possible to see, in this dimly lit area, that Sunnylawn was hardly a house and grounds anymore. The grounds were chewed into small bits on which crouched buildings not much bigger than dog kennels, even if they were occasionally two-storied. But above them loomed a building. Alan recognized, at last, the barn where old Montgraine had kept his flashy trotters. He walked further, through a maze of tiny streets and over a slippery crust of garbage and mud, to find the house itself, apparently intact, rearing above him.

His heart skipped. Many of the windows were lighted and how familiar it looked! He outdistanced his guide-light bearer and came around the corner to the front porch. He was a little startled to find the place enclosed, for the verandah had been large and one of the principal beauties of the house. But he went swiftly to the door.

Surging optimism placed no slightest doubt between him and the rack of cards he found there. He swept aside this obvious evidence that the place had been chopped into apartments and lighting his lighter, against all rules of the Light Bearers' Guild, he found her name!

"Miss Cerita Montgraine."

Well!

He whirled on the bearer, gave him a bill hit or miss from his roll, told him a happy goodbye and pressed hard on the bell.

He waited. He straightened up his jacket, adjusted his collar, wished he had taken a moment to remove some of the stain of the *Hound*, realized how grimy his jacket was and took it off.

Apprehensively he punched the bell a second time. He was not worried. It was not really late yet. She would be up.

Chica. Well, he'd have to do some fast explaining at being gone so long. And he'd be very well braced against seeing her older than he had really expected. Make her as old as could be. That was all right. It was his fault and they could tie something together and make a life of it. What if she was even forty-five or fifty. That was all right. A woman needed some age to take proper care of a man. Who had said that? Queen? Funny old Queen. And he'd been up there where the stars were shining and he'd thought he'd never get back. What an entire fool he was. Jocelyn was right. He was a fool. He'd figured he'd never get back and here it was right on the bell, "Miss Cerita Montgraine." And how he'd watched that speed dial!

He wished he'd taken a little more time. He had mud on his shoes. Water wasn't plenty on a long passage. Well, she'd understand all that. She'd waited, hadn't she? She'd waited!

And there were footsteps on the porch within and the door opened a slit.

Alan beamed and got ready to grab her in his arms.

But it was a sad-faced little dwarf of a man, and he said, "Go away."

Alan chuckled. What a ragged tramp he must look. "I am sorry, I have no card to send in. But I'm a friend."

He couldn't resist the surprise factors involved in it. How she'd laugh with him.

"No friends. If you want money, no money."

Alan blocked the door from being shut. He grinned good-humoredly. "Truly I *am* a friend. An *old* friend."

"Nope. Take your foot out." The man was frightened.

Hang it, he'd have to forgo the surprise. Maybe it was better. He'd scare her enough, turning up from the dead. "Don't be afraid. Nobody is going to hurt you. Announce"—he drew a breath—"Mr. Alan Corday."

The dwarf peered near-sightedly in the dimness. "You ain't government?"

"No, truly I assure you I am not."

"This ain't no trick? 'Cause if it is, I got some sharp medicine I give to them that's ailin'."

"Friend, this is no trick. Your mistress will know me instantly."

"Well, I doubt that. But, keepin' in mind my sharp medicine, you can come up."

"I think you had better announce me first."

"She's ready to be looked at," said the dwarf. "And you mind the medicine." He opened the door and hobbled across the porch and up the stairs.

At the back of the house he stopped and swung open a panel. He looked in, nodded to himself and said, "Miss Chica. Miss Chica! Gentleman to see you callin' himself Mr. Alan Corday. Miss Chica, you wake up. Gentleman to see you."

A thin little voice answered him. "I'm awake, Saib. I'm not in bed, am I? Of course I'm awake. I'm dressed so I'm not in bed."

"Gentleman to—"

"Here, let me!" said Alan, and thrust the panel wide.

He was not certain what he saw, after the first glance. Afterwards he could not recall where she had sat or how she had looked.

There was a mantel with some crockery on it, some overcrowded tables with china dogs and horses on them, several heavy chairs and a very narrow, covered bed.

"Is it going to rain? All day long I have felt it was going to rain. It isn't raining, is it?"

TO THE STARS

L. RON HUBBARD

122

"Gentleman to see you!" Saib insisted sharply. "You got to talk up, mister. She don't hear well. But she's sprightly. Dresses herself."

"Oh, yes, of course, how foolish of me. Well, sir. See you now. Do be seated. And what was the name?"

Saib said, "Mr. Alan Corday."

There was a brief, puzzled silence. And then, "But he isn't in."

Alan sat down on a frail little rocking chair.

"He isn't here," she repeated in some distress, twisting her tiny, shriveled hands together.

"Mister, don't you go frettin' her," said Saib menacingly. "She's a tenth class but she's got her amnesty, because of her mind, you know. Recollect what I said about medicine and don't fret her."

"I was just about to have tea," she said. "Saib, bring in the tea things and serve the gentleman. I know I am dreadfully impolite not to be more hospitable, but ever since my husband died I have kept alone pretty much, you see. You knew him? A fine man. So strong and handsome. And such a way with him. He was an engineer-surveyor and when he came back we were married. You'd have liked him. I don't see very well but you look young. Are you young, sir? Excuse an inquisitive old lady, but perhaps you knew one of our sons in school. Ah, there's the tea. You'll have one lump or two?"

Saib put down the tray. It was a barren tray. A heel of bread, a tiny pat of butter and a teapot. She poured shakily and sought to place his cup beside him. Saib quickly assisted her an instant before disaster.

"Heavens, you'd think I couldn't do a thing," she said. "But you were telling me about one of my sons. Was it Raymond? What a good boy he is. Writes me every week. You do think he's handsome, don't you?"

She sipped at her tea and set it aside. "It does feel like rain. Was it raining out when you came in? I keep feeling it is going to rain, Saib. Is it raining yet?"

"No, miss. It's not raining," said Saib. "Maybe you didn't hear. This is Mr. Corday."

Her hands shook badly as she lifted the teacup. She appeared to be very confused, peering about her, shaking her head slightly, trying to reach some memory.

"Oh," she said with relief, "you mean young Alan. Why, young man, I'm awfully sorry. Young Alan just isn't at home. He went out about an hour ago with some girl. Heavens, what a dangerous man he is. Broken hearts and the best families. But he'll settle down. Don't you worry about any son of mine, sir. They'll all be a credit to their father. All of them, sir. All of them."

Alan was standing, tearing at his cap.

"Oh, do you have to go so soon? And it's such good tea tonight. Real tea, but Saib is such a dear child. Can't you stay until Alan returns? Until Alan returns? Until Alan returns?"

"Here, here," said Saib. "You are spilling your tea and getting the rug all wet. You better go, sir. The old lady won't take excitement. Her heart, you understand. And she's had a mighty promisin' day so far."

"Goodbye," she said brightly. "Goodbye and do call again. I so enjoyed your news about young Alan. Saib, have them bring around a car for Alan's friend. It might rain, you know. Goodbye, sir. Goodbye."

Saib took him to the outer door. "She has her good days and her bad, good and bad. Today's a good one. The doctor'll be happy to hear it when he comes tomorrow. He's an old white like myself—drove for Greeson Graham in the old days, I did, and would have paid for it with my neck if they hadn't needed somebody to tend what was left of the stables. Then the doctor two years back talked them into letting me take care of the old woman there. Got to liking her right well. Funny old sort. You wouldn't know what happened to her, would you? I mean what drove her mad? Well, maybe it was the revolution. It got a lot of them. But somebody said she was crazy even before that and they didn't execute her because . . . well, I don't know. She's a good sort and she doesn't talk much. Most words I ever heard her speak was tonight. And I feel better serving a tenth class. Used to their style, I guess. But don't take no truck about her family. Shucks. She wasn't ever married and she sure hasn't got any sons."

He opened the door for Alan. "Here, what's this? Money? Say, this is an awful lot. Well, the old lady can use some food, that I guarantee. Say, this is a lot of money! Well, you can trust me to stretch it out, though I guess she hasn't got much more time. Must be eighty now. I don't get you, sir. You never said what you come for. What did you come for, mister? This money?"

Alan, two hours later, found himself walking in the rain she had feared. It was a heavy rain and it soaked his white jacket through and through.

He stood for moments and looked at the lowering sky, gray in the lights of the town.

She had said she thought it would rain.

CHAPTER 12

The quivering *Hound of Heaven* hurled herself on course, blazing bow to bridge with particle flame, drives snarling with subdued ferocity as they sped to higher speeds, a lance of fire in the black of absolute zero.

In two ship-years the bridge had not changed much. There was a new communicator man on his watch, the old one dead in a fight on the Capella System; the glass had broken all the way out of the speed dial; and Swifty sometimes shook now as he relieved the watch. But otherwise it was the same—a belt of black ports through which one saw the march of stars, a worn deck which was never washed, panel on panel and rack on rack of meters, dials and controls, scummed each one with grease.

Alan leaned against the rail in the wing, fingers hooked in the spaceman's habit of never going far from a handhold and never being unprepared against ungravity. It was the secured watch with a minimum crew on stations. An hour since they had "piped the belly," and the food smell was still strong in the ship but weakening as the blower filters cleaned the always foul air; and the crowd, a hundred and fifty-some strong, was in the mess hall still, having an impromptu sing.

The quartermaster had left the ladder open so that they could hear on the bridge and up floated the exultant strains of "Viva la Company."

A *friend on the left and a friend on the right,*
Viva la company.
In *hale and good fellowship let us unite,*
Viva la company.
Viva la viva la viva la Hound
Viva la viva la viva la Hound
Viva la Hound *viva la* Hound
Viva la company.

The steersman started to hum it into the ensuing quiet. "Silence on the bridge," said Alan Corday.

The throb of the big ship seemed louder and more intense at the song's end and the belt of ports was blacker. Alan looked at the speed dial. They were rushing upwards now to one hundred and fifty thousand miles a second. They would have their speed in a few more watches. She was always uneven through the hundred forties and he was glad to be out of them. The Deuce thought it was a fault in her fuel catalysts. Ever since these new drives had been installed ten trips ago she'd had that characteristic. But she was beating at it now. One could barely see the needle move. It was less tiring on the crew through the hundred fifties and up, for one's weight eased down as the gravity curve decreased. But she had to work for it and one could feel her throbbing by touching his finger to the rail.

They were singing again, "The Spaceman's Dream." And Alan beat slow time to it with his pencil, delaying a change course compute for spatial curve until the song was done.

He had made some progress in his navigation in two years. All the minor computations he did now. But his ears still burned when he thought of Jocelyn's discovery of a tenth of a second error in his compute one day.

"I don't misdoubt, Mr. Corday, that some day when I am old and bent you'll have mastered simple trig. Mr. Hale, loan Mr. Corday a book on sphericals. You won't need one on arithmetic too, will you, Mr. Corday?"

He stabbed the pencil into the pad recalling it and looked up half expecting to see Gow-eater close by, on guard. But Gow-eater was a suicide these past eight months, and Alan, while very far from third in command, went about his work alone.

As the song finished he looked again at the speed dial and then to the course checkers and began his compute for curve.

They began to sing "Voyage," timed to the thud of drives.

Up into the darkling sky
The Hound her bow has reared,
Up against the cold, clean stars
Her course is set and steered.

And high above Capella looms,
A pinpoint in the sky,
While drivers throb and meters bob
A thousand years will die.

The captain he has checked the course,

The mates are standing by,
We'll take our chance with meteors
And check commands gone by.

We'll stand out to Capella's glare
And thunder at the black
And lance the way and never stay
Until we've made the rack.

The daylight's thin behind us now,
The careless stars are dim,
The weakest of the Circus crew
Is certain that we'll win.

A full ten times a hundred years
Will pass as on we run,
A full ten times a hundred years
Earth spins around the Sun.

Then back we'll be with ore and gem
Enough a town to buy,
The Hound but six months older now
For only planets die.

God bless the mates
And keep our crew from harm upon this day,
And God bless Captain Jocelyn
Who walks his lonely way.

Alan squirmed a little. The song was very old and, as it died away, he was conscious suddenly of how slightly he belonged, how casual was their acceptance of him. With a sudden shock he realized that in more than two years of cruising he had not made a friend.

He was Mr. Corday, the young man who might someday become third in command, someone to be obedient to by duty and custom, someone to consult on routine matters, the person to see when you wanted minor hull repairs.

But he knew suddenly that he had never belonged. Wrapped in his own griefs and dismays, he had forgotten the ship. And he looked back now over the last two years with the strange sensation that he had never been quite within the hull.

There were reasons for it, he told himself quickly. There was the matter of mutiny. Not the one Queen had contemplated, but one which had almost won, engaged upon by five new men taken on Venus from a wrecked system-liner crew. He went shaky even now when he recalled the apprehension of them and the execution.

Jocelyn, with the crew assembled except for a skeleton watch, had read quietly out of a small book called the *Holy Bible*, had dropped a dispassionate hand and one by one, without suits, the five had been dropped from an air lock into the instant extinction of vacuum and absolute zero.

He recalled suddenly the conversation between Gow-eater and Mag Godine.

"But they froze first!" Mag had said. "So they don't explode."

"They explode first," Gow-eater had answered heatedly. "They never get a chance to freeze."

"I tell you," said Mag, "that they go floating around like planets, froze stiff."

"And I tell you," Gow-eater had said, "that they become, instanter and without delay, a pale pink mist of plain ordinary atoms. So there!"

They'd never settled it. Odd that they, who had been so long in space, with ample examples to cite, had brought no facts into the argument. It had ended with personal recriminations and Mistress Mag had not spoken to anyone for days.

And watching them it had come belatedly to Alan how narrowly close he had come to that same fate. It had made him very humble to Jocelyn, the thought of it. And to this day he had never spoken to either Strange or Queen without a surge of shame.

Not fear, he realized suddenly, standing here on watch, listening to a new song—shame. For Jocelyn had picked him up and brought him back that time after his first trip and Jocelyn had been almost kind. And he had once been a partner to a plan which would have murdered, as its very first step, Captain Jocelyn.

He was suddenly nervous about it again. He did not understand Jocelyn, but then nobody did. Strange, cold Jocelyn, always meticulously dressed in white, always biting, never affected by anything. Jocelyn and his whiskey and headache powder. Jocelyn and his command of strange and ancient music. Jocelyn and his sixth sense about the ship. And Jocelyn, ruthless, without principles or ethics or morals—Alan understood no part of him. And he detested the man entire.

They began to sing "Why, Why, Why Do We Cruise the Useless Sky," and Alan, for the thousandth time faced that. And as it rolled, rollicking, satirical, poking ridicule at one and all, he again felt the never-quite-absent surge of desperation.

They had no purpose. They had no goal. They were outcasts, condemned to exist until they died without home or friends behind the skin of this vessel, accomplishing nothing, idly watching the parade of the pointless centuries. Why?

Toward the end of the watch Hale wandered up full of dinner and songs sung, smoking a terrible cigar, to check their position of advance, always an uncertain thing before speed was attained. Alan watched him for a little while.

"Well, looks like we'll be on Earth again in about nine hundred watches," Hale complacently roared to the bridge in general.

Alan spoke up suddenly: "Why?"

Bucko Hale looked at him in astonishment. He gawped for a moment and then, about to lose his cigar, worked it over to the other side of his huge mouth.

"We could have stayed on that last planet," said Alan.

"Could have—" began Hale, wits accelerating slowly.

"Water, game, timber, fine climate, no dangers,

small colony already started. I looked it over. Didn't you?"

"Stayed on . . . on O'Rourke?" said Hale.

"Why not? We could do worse. We've got odds and ends of the crafts aboard. We have a government. And we could live our lives like people."

"Live our lives—? What are you? Drunk?"

"Give me a good reason against it."

"Why, why . . . there's plenty against it. I—" And he floundered and began to get angry because he didn't have an answer.

"We play tag with disaster every trip. We'll get back to Earth now and who knows what we'll find. Certainly things will have changed in the fifty generations we've been gone. We'll have no more common ground with Earth this time than we had last. They don't want us. They've got no use for us. When we get a cargo they'll clip us badly because they know that not even their great-great-great-grandchildren will ever lay eyes on us. We serve no planet in the stars that really needs us. Now tell me why we didn't stay on O'Rourke and live like men."

Hale looked irritably around and drew himself up toward the explosion point. "You tryin' to breed discontent? If you don't like to make a good liberty, then some people do. If you don't like sport and plenty of money, that don't mean we're all little gents. And," he cried, his voice rising and strained, "if you don't like it, hit dirt next stop! You don't have to stay aboard!"

And Hale departed.

Alan had stiffened at the last blast. He stood now, crimson, furious. He knew they could do without him. Jocelyn said it often enough. He knew he didn't really belong. But it was not fair of Hale to strike so hard with it in answer to a simple question.

But was it simple? When he thought of his last trip in he wondered. The language had changed so much that he had been very poorly understood. For that matter, he wasn't even speaking good English by this time but ship patois and "on dirt," trade pidgin, the timeless lingua spacia. His own technology was thirty-five hundred years forgotten and rusty on Earth. To fit himself into that society now he would have to start in the first grade and study everything from grammar to manners. He did not belong on Earth anymore. He was homeless, a wanderer in absolute zero and eternity. But Hale need not have driven it so hard.

He frowned. Jocelyn liked his creature comforts.

Why didn't Jocelyn see how really easy it would be to make a new colony of his ship on some hospitable star? Earth, no. But a good planet in an astronomically reliable system—why not?

And then he recalled the brutality of some of their visits and the greed and licenses of the crew. Those, he thought, disheartened, were answers.

CHAPTER 13

She's a bloomin' antique," said the yard superintendent, "but I think she can be patched." Alan was somewhat astonished to find himself nettled at the attitude of this shirt-sleeved Earthman. It seemed to him, each trip, that the race was not quite as vital as the last time he had contacted it. And this slur against the *Hound*, whatever the curses Alan himself gave her, was not to be tolerated from such plebeian lips. He got out the first syllable of a biting rejoinder and then altered his tone in midflight. No professional ethics were ever used on a long-passage ship, not in any age, and the lives of all aboard might depend upon the goodwill of this fellow.

"I am sure you can do something," said Alan. "Of course, as usual, you won't have any spare parts for her machinery, but I think we can reinstall whole units where any spare parts are required."

The yard superintendent looked suspiciously at him. "You're just a young fellow to be talking so handsome. You got authority for such expenditure? It'll come to a fine piece of money."

"I am in charge of construction," said Alan, holding hard to his temper. "And I have authority to expend any necessary sums for her repairs."

"Hm-m-m. Now you take that hole in her bow, there. These old false-nose jobs aren't so easy to patch up. Have to remove all the collision packing to get meteor chunks out, if any, and build up new braces and coilspring bulkheads . . . cost . . . hm-m-m," a calculating glance at Alan, "cost around, say, hundred and twenty thousand tylers, more or less."

Alan pulled out a small book and made a pencil calculation on the flyleaf. He could not convert various currency changes and his engineering had been taught to him in dollars. He used the price of a dish of ham and eggs as his medium of conversion, those having cost, in the average restaurant, about a dollar in his time. This proposed repair was then about thirty thousand dollars, according to his check of the local spaceport restaurant.

"Thirty thousand," he muttered. "Can't do business for more than a hundred thousand tylers."

"Have to skimp the work," said the yard superintendent dolefully.

"Even," said Alan, lowering his voice, "if you get a personal two thousand tylers on satisfactory completion?"

The superintendent glanced swiftly around and then winked. "You long-passage johnnies got a whole book of tricks. Draggin' the ages."

Half the conversation he heard, even when it was conducted in what they called lingua spacia in the professorial handbooks, was beyond him now. Alan was developing the unconscious conviction that wherever he went he dwelt with foreigners. He would have contested this in an argument, for it is a foolish idea indeed to have one's country, socialistically, linguistically and ethnologically, all contained in a metal hull.

"Now there's the matter of air tanks," he said. "I suppose you have something new in filters or motors."

The superintendent grew cunning. What they called the mechanical renaissance was hard upon Earth and secondhand equipment was easy to find, so rapidly were designs changed. He knew of some old units he could get cheap—last year's. Alan looked them over, puzzled out their principle, finally studied out that they broke air into individual atoms and used the unwanted impurities for power. Then he deduced that there must be newer equipment from the signs of material progress he saw all about him, demanded it and secured it, shining in its packing crates.

"This afternoon," said Alan, having settled price on this, "I will run up to New Chicago and get checking estimates. I—"

"To where?"

Alan turned and looked north to where the city sprawled, sixteen levels high, suburbs extending eight hundred miles all about.

"You mean Candia," said the superintendent. "I recollect somebody sayin' there was another town here once, but Candia's been around—let me see—darned if I know. Maybe six, seven hundred years. Real old. We got some buildings they say go clear back to the Third Triarchy. Oldest in Halloland."

"Where?"

"Halloland, the continent."

"You mean North America."

"Can't say as I ever heard of that. But about these estimates. You can trust me. Point is, can I trust you?"

"Don't worry about pay," said Alan. "We were unloading half the morning, or didn't you notice?"

"Sure, but unloading what? You long-passage boys get some mighty peculiar ideas about cargo sometimes. Saw a ship in here last May on your crazy business and she'd brought rocks. Just plain rocks."

"Must have been more than that," said Alan. "Nobody would haul rocks fifty or a hundred light-years."

"Yep, rocks. We had a lot of trouble with that outfit. They was crazy as loons, the whole lot. Claimed the stuff was called uranium."

"Had a use once," defended Alan.

"You couldn't prove it by me. We looked it up in every book in sight and couldn't even find it. I got a whole library out of the *Wanderbar IV*, thousand-year-old stuff. Swapped the skipper even, sold half as rare books, kept the engineering. And no uranium. Just rocks."

"But what do you use as fuel?" said Alan.

"Sand."

Alan blinked. "Well, took 'em a long time. Low-order fission, well, well."

"Low-order what?"

"Fission."

"Brother, we ain't got it."

"How do you burn the sand?"

"Pour cataphan on it. Runs about two million H.T.U. of heat to the jig."

"What's an H.T.U. and what's a jig? And what's this cataphan?"

"Sonny, I ain't got time to teach school today. Swap you a complete handbook and a dictionary for that gun you're packing. Be quite a find to the museum. They really hang around me in case you boys may come in. Got a flag one day off a ship called *Molly Murphy*. Red, white and blue. Stars. Pretty. They'd been half across the galaxy, I guess. Six thousand years or so. Price they got for the junk they had aboard made up for the cargo of diamonds. Six tons of diamonds. They're over there on the other side of that shed. You got any more of those guns, I'll swap you two burners, brand-new, for each."

"And a burner?"

"Side pistol you'd say. Two thousand rounds. Cataphan."

"What's this cataphan?"

"Here, come in," and he took Alan into the shed office. He picked up a phial and held it to the light. It contained perhaps a quarter of an ounce.

"That's a jig of cataphan. Two thousand tylers' worth. They get this stuff out of Pluto. It's an ore extract. Here, give me the gun and you can have the books here. Read?"

"Make a try," said Alan.

"Well, here's a dictionary in and out of lingua spacia. Had them made up by the museum to accommodate you boys. Maybe six or eight of you come in here a year and while our main business is the Saturn Line and the Sun Excursion Company, we got to be accommodatin'. Got the only old racks that will take you boys anywhere on the continent. And we mean to oblige. Now this bill you mean to run up here is around two million tylers. You sure you'll have cash?"

"We brought in an eight-billion-tyler cargo of furs," said Alan.

"What kind?"

"Lotus of Mizar puronic."

"Gosh. You did? Say, you boys must not care what you do. And that's smart. I seen one once on a ritocrat's girlfriend. All yours gold?"

"Some scarlet taken in the cold season."

"Hey now, don't let yourselves get skidded. My guess is they're worth twenty billion if anybody ordered eight, just on the principle. Women will be women."

"What's this cataphan's ore?" said Alan.

"There in the book. Small deposit on Pluto, only one known. Here's a chunk of the ore. Like to help you boys out if—"

"Whew!" said Alan, unbending in his excitement.

"Ahah! You've seen it?"

"A mountain of it, shedding lava."

"That ore is worth five hundred tylers a jig. Here, have a smoke?"

Alan reached for the box and it was almost withdrawn.

"Go ahead. But I just remembered that I won't even be dust when you come in here again. But have a cigar anyway. After all, we'll be making ten percent of two million off you boys. Go ahead and have two cigars."

Alan made the final arrangements for racking the ship in the morning and hastened up the gangway. Most of the crew was "on dirt," spending. But Snoozer was sitting inside the lock.

"Jocelyn aboard?"

"He's got some people up there," said Snoozer, brushing out the folds of a scarf she had wheeled out of a peddler. "Are you going townside, Mr. Corday?"

But Alan was up the ladder and into the big cabins in a rush. He had the ore in one hand, the dictionary and engineering book in the other. "Sir—"

"And I assure you, gentlemen," continued Jocelyn blandly, "that no other spot is so admirably suited to a colony. Good air, unit gravity, edible plants, Earthlike animal life. Johnny's Landing is, I am sure, the ideal place."

Alan stopped still, unable to believe what he heard. His own recollection of Johnny's Landing was pungent with death and disappointment. He stood back.

"This is Mr. Corday," said Jocelyn, "our second mate. A most talented and accomplished young engineer, a good example of the high caliber of our personnel. Regiment Hauber, Mr. Corday."

Alan found himself shaking hands with a white-haired, serene-faced old man who, in turn, introduced him to the four other members of the party.

"Your Captain Jocelyn," said Regiment Hauber, in

halting lingua spacia, obviously but newly learned, "has been acquainting us with some of the prospects. Now what do you think of Johnny's Landing for a new colony, young man?"

Alan started to speak in a rush, but he was halted by a flash in Jocelyn's usually languid eye.

"He thinks highly of it," said Jocelyn. "He was once there. These gentlemen head up a potential colony, Mr. Corday. We may have the pleasure of carrying them and their equipment. Now tell these gentlemen frankly what you know of Johnny's Landing. Is it fertile?"

"Yes, I—"

"And unit gravity?"

"Of course, but—"

"And you saw no animals except those useful to man?"

"No, they—"

"And water and air were good?" said Regiment Hauber.

"Of course. But I—"

"What were you going to say, Mr. Corday?" said Jocelyn. "Go on and tell the gentlemen."

Alan bit his lip. His wits were for a moment frozen by Jocelyn's presence and then suddenly they whirred with answers. There was a very faint mockery in Alan's voice when he replied. "I am certain that these gentlemen would find Johnny's Landing a splendid place, sir. The very best sort of place. But perhaps the captain will not be so agreeable when he learns something I have just discovered."

Alan put down the bit of ore and the handbook. "You can ask these gentlemen about cataphan, sir. It has displaced everything—uranium, coal, oil, thermalon—" He urged it into Jocelyn's hand. "And it is worth two thousand dollars an ounce."

Jocelyn looked up from the ore, eyes narrowing as he studied Alan, and then he thumbed at the handbook. Alan smiled at the old man and his friends. He had liked them on sight—sincere, quixotic with idealism, trusting the whole Universe and bound outwards on colonization, which in itself said much. Most colonists were convicts, political refugees, defeated nationals or the eugenic outcasts. Once in a very long time such a man as Regiment Hauber and his friends undertook the gamble of outer space. Earth had neither encouragement nor discouragement to offer. Occasionally she exported unwanted to the stars— once, sometime back, she had loaded up the remaining half of a defeated Venusian rebel navy and had sent them outward bound. Alan had met one of the ships on No. 5 Sun[16], the vessel now in the trade of the long passage. It was this gesture of contempt on the part of Earth which brought to him how little Earth had to fear from colonies.

Regiment Hauber might or might not know the truth about other systems. But a colony, laid down anywhere out there, could not expect intelligence of its whereabouts to return for generations. News would not circulate widely in the vessels of the long passage for more than a handful of millenniums. No other ships would stop unless the planet was rich. It was abandonment complete and isolation utter, a somewhat frightening prospect even to a brave man.

Earth did not care to plant colonies since there was no short-term advantage. But so far it had not objected in the least to colonies being planted. Predicating their philosophy on a continued advance of Earth culture, the succeeding governments on Earth knew that nothing was to be feared from an attack from outer space. Many hostile and even terrible races had been discovered out amongst the stars, but none with enough technology to conquer or attempt to conquer space. Further, any attack on Earth by a colony in the stars using Earth culture would find itself hundreds of years, perhaps, behind Earth culture in terms of weapons and ships. Taking the latest with him, Regiment Hauber would be thirty years behind technology on Earth the instant he landed on Johnny's Landing. Even an already founded colony, taking the latest technical information from some ship on the long passage, could not build up an effective offensive force which would compete with Earth. And an attacker from some star would have to compose itself of soldiers very desperate indeed to leave their homes forever behind them—for any force from any star would not return home in time to resume concourse with their peoples.

Earth, then, did not object to any such activity. It cared little about the long passage. It cared not at all about Regiment Haubers and their optimistic people. The drain on Earth population in this manner was minute but welcome—Earth, as Alan had discovered that morning, now numbering its peoples at ten for every arable acre, about one hundred sixty percent of what current agriculture could provide.

But there were few volunteers for the long

passage. At least few who had the money to go and the desperation to attempt it, for desperation is no handmaid of cash.

"I trust you will have good equipment, sir," said Alan, to break the silence of Jocelyn's study.

Hauber smiled benignly. "We have the very best, Mr. Corday. The very best. But of course we'll need the advice of old hands such as yourselves and we'll follow your advices. You know what it is like out there. We don't."

Jocelyn looked up alertly. "I recall the place you have in mind, Mr. Corday. I recall it very well. And I recall the mountain. It was undoubtedly this ore in contact with silica at the base. Thank you for your interest in the matter."

Alan started to smile; for once he had got the edge on Jocelyn. But he checked the smile with the realization that Jocelyn never thanked anybody for anything unless he had something else in mind.

"Very instructive," Jocelyn continued. "But if the Pluto deposit is so small, I don't doubt but what they'll have had to find a newer fuel by the time we return. Mr. Corday is rather young, gentlemen. Excuse his bursting in here with this bric-a-brac. You may leave, Mr. Corday.

And if you find any new marvels, pray don't fail to report them. Don't fail."

Alan gave him a glare of pure hate and quickly about-faced. As he left the room he heard the smooth voice of Jocelyn saying, "Now, gentlemen, about this venture. We can take five hundred, if you don't mind crowding. We're having new air supplies installed of a very late pattern and, after all, it's only a few weeks. But I would advise you to cut your number in favor of freight. Three hundred women, one hundred men. It happens that I know of a cache on Johnny's Landing which might be useful, but freight, after all, is the important item. Besides, at ten thousand tylers the passenger—"

Snoozer was still at the air lock. Alan scarcely saw her, such was his bitterness over this venture. Ten thousand tylers the passenger. And a high bill for freight. And half a dozen of the best young men shipped forever and the prettiest women detained and a colony planted where a colony had suddenly perished before—

"Are you going to hit dirt?" said Snoozer. "I have six of these funny tylers to—"

"The man's a devil," said Alan with heat. "A devil! A

devil!" And he walked angrily down the gangway and out of sight while Snoozer, drooping, her new scarf not so pretty to her now, looked after him through misting eyes.

CHAPTER 14

*B*ehold the funny passenger
Afloat in thinnest air
Missing on all gravities
His coffee in his hair . . .

"Ye gods," finished Queen, "I'll be happy when we can get this ship cleaned out."

Alan looked at her across the wardroom table with a shudder of distaste. She put down the tray of bottles she had brought up from Marby's greasy lair and smoothed her dyed hair.

Swifty laughed and reached for his quart. "Good sport, the women though, what?" he said.

"You young dog, you," said Queen. "Your own people not good enough for you. When are you going to take up regular, dearie? My shoes have been outside my door for years."

"The only thing which keeps me back," said Swifty, "is a frightful respect of that bally knife old Marby carries, dear. Tiri-liri-tura-lu, first one today."

"First bottle, you mean," said Queen. "Well, I'll have to carry on the picture of unrequited love, honey. Here are your cigarettes, Mr. Corday."

Alan broke the seal on the pack and selected one. They were getting hard to come by. Nobody in the Solar System, it seemed, had smoked them for centuries. He scribbled his name on the chit and handed it back.

Queen took it coolly, lifted the tray and with a rumple through Swifty's hair, departed.

It was a little gesture. Alan listened to her receding heelbeats. Suddenly, as she had smiled at Swifty, Alan knew how very lonely he was. He had neither liking nor respect for Queen, for her brawls with Marby, for her native unscrubbedness—for even after he had installed the re-use system for water a couple of trips ago, making unlimited water available, Queen, too long in space, had stayed unwashed. He winced at her bawdy jokes and at her familiarities with everyone from apprentice spaceman to Hale. But, he had realized abruptly, she was still part of the ship, part of his country. And like his country and his ship, she now ignored him.

He lighted the precious smoke and found it had no flavor. He looked at Swifty, lounging at the foot of the table, soaking up coffee royal in a moment stolen from the bridge with Jocelyn, for once on his proper watch. Swifty was goodhearted to everyone and yet even Swifty seemed distant to him.

"Swifty," he said suddenly, meaning to go on and ask his question.

"Eh?"

"Nothing."

"Oh."

Alan twisted around uncomfortably and looked the other way. He knew he had a lot of things to overcome. He had a manner which had been born into him— abrupt, aloof as became a tenth class. He knew he had a lot of failings in his association with his fellow man. It was not easy to be here, in this variegated company, and have no single intimate. Couldn't he forget he was a tenth class? Maybe that was what was wrong with him. A tenth class— But where was the tenth class now? Not any on Earth but the most learnedly profound professor of ancient history knew what a tenth class had been now. How did a man shed his background? Could he do so?

Strange, ingratiating to all, even Alan, had said something one night about wiping out experience from the mind. Strange had claimed that an ancient work he had seen in his youth gave forth a method which would eradicate even loyalty from the mind. If he could just forget— But he shuddered at the vision of some of the crew, empty-eyed people on whom Strange had worked. He turned back and was about to ask Swifty what the crew thought of him when his cigarettes, which had been floating upwards from ungravity, fell with a crash into his empty coffee cup. He started up, as the whole crew always did with a change in the vessel, and then sank back.

"Check blasting for a land, what?" said Swifty. "Thirty watches we'll be in and then, heigh-ho, to work we go. That young Bill the Eye will do the work though. Jolly good joke. He's so crazy about piloting he hasn't found out yet what hard work it is."

This interested Alan. "Who gave you authority? Why, he's just a child. Twelve, isn't he?"

"Fine pilot. Bit reckless though. Buzzed a parade

last look-see on Earth. Had to bat him to make him stop. Born flyboy."

"You mean he's got whole control? Swifty, Bill isn't big enough to see out of a cockpit."

"Got to start 'em sometime," said Swifty.

"But the plane. That's the only one we've got!"

Swifty sat up. "Oh, bosh, Corday. Come off it and try to live like us mortals." And Swifty, good-natured Swifty, took up his bottle and left the wardroom without a backward glance.

Alan glared at the pilot's back and then, after a moment, slumped, staring with hurt eyes into his empty cup.

Snoozer, big-eyed, clean-scrubbed, hesitated outside the door. Then she rapped with a burst of courage. "Cap'n's compliments, Mr. Corday, and he wants a navigational check."

Alan rose and walked past her to the ladder which led down to the bridge.

"You forgot your cigarettes, Mr. Corday," said Snoozer, snatching them up.

He took them and went on.

CHAPTER 15

Johnny's Landing presented a slightly altered aspect. It was speckled with farms and cities, laked with artificial dams and netted with something Alan recognized as ancient power lines. This—to the *Hound*—sudden change was extremely disagreeable to Jocelyn.

Jocelyn's face was bone-white with hatred as he stood on the bridge, binoculars clenched in a savage hand. It startled Alan that the pleasant prospect of the domed little cities which stretched out of the hilltop on which they had landed could so affect the captain. And then Alan took down his own binoculars from the rack and inspected for himself.

The hill on which they stood was some five hundred feet above the plain. And the bridge of the *Hound* reared three hundred and eighty feet above her tail so that the view was very fine.

But in three seconds of looking with his binoculars

at fifty power, Alan saw, though with much less emotion, what Jocelyn had beheld. There was a small army, headed by half a dozen tanks and followed by artillery, coming up the road from the nearest city.

But they were not men.

"Corday!" snapped Jocelyn, strained white with ferocity, "take a party of twenty with hand weapons and attack!"

Alan stared for an instant at Jocelyn and then looked back at the horde. It must number half a thousand with reinforcements running in across fields. Then he saw the antiquity of the weapons.

"Aye, aye, sir," he said. And five minutes later he was going down the hill to a defile in the rocks a mile and a half from the ship, twenty crewmen at his back and Bill the Eye skipping along beside him in a high quiver of excitement, elated and crowing at having been grabbed up as a messenger.

"Seen 'em when I was about five," said Bill, tow hair standing straight up. "The Earth colony here used 'em as slaves. Then they all died off from something. But you was here when we landed the last time. Guess in the thousands of years since I was ten they sprung out of someplace again."

Alan was appraising the oncoming forces. He swept his men into double-time and threw them into position on either side of the road in the defile, ready with an enfilade hand fire when the range was two miles.

"Old Jocelyn's death on these sentient races," chattered Bill. "Seen him burn down five hundred thousand Gleenites oncet. Burned 'em clean off Majority Capella. That was before your time. You got any chewin' gum?"

Watching that crawling snake of an army, Alan shuddered a little. It was a chilly thing. These "people" had no features or eyes that he could see through his glass. Then he shifted to their nearest town and then to a power line. Strange but those things were quite different from anything he had ever seen in the ancient histories of Earth. With sudden amazement he shifted back to the oncoming army. The things could evolve a society that included finite physics. And then a slight chill hit him. If they could get this far, they could someday throw ships into the long passage. And that army showed they had no slightest use for man.

"You goin' to pile 'em up all at once?" said Bill. "Or pick 'em off at long range?"

Alan ignored him. He took a pocket ranger out and

sighted in a far white boulder at one and a quarter miles. He passed the data along to his tensely waiting spacemen.

On came the brown snake through the dust. The leading tanks breasted the white boulder. Eyes were on Alan's hand as he raised it. On came the snake, swelling as things wriggled over walls and dropped into the road to march on with it.

Half the snake passed the white boulder. With a short, vicious chop, Alan brought down his arm. The defile crackled, the air ionized, the daylight went dim.

There was a shudder in the center of the snake. And the air crackled on. Dust, and smoke from ignited pavement, curled upwards, speared lazily into the sky and obscured the slaughter. The pall grew dense, grew black, grew inner-lit with red tonguing flames. The valley was full of stench and smoke.

And then, suddenly, a hundred yards to their front emerged from out the rolling clouds three tanks. Tubes from them were bucking and leaping and spitting scarlet. Rock splinters flew upward before Alan's face and he fell back, stunned. The spacemen, firing still at range given, wildly readjusted their hand weapons. And a tank churned in amongst them.

There was a crash from the ship as its forward battery fired, rending the air overhead into green tatters. Bill the Eye snatched at Alan's sidearm, threw over its catch, and just as the tank turned to depress its muzzles, Bill shot.

There was an explosive boil of molten metal and fragments of a blazing thing. Bill fired again for good measure.

Two hours later Alan, wearing a bandage, stood to on the quiet bridge, waiting for Jocelyn. Alan knew what he was going to be told. He had erred in not picking off the armor in the van and in forgetting it could come forward at high speed under cover of the smoke and dust. He had had one crewman killed because of it. And he had been rescued by young Bill the Eye, a messenger.

Jocelyn had been down conferring with Regiment Hauber as they disembarked to take possession of a countryside which was a going concern—if potentially depopulated by Swifty's quick flight with virus over the towns of these hideous things.

At last Jocelyn came up on the bridge. Alan stiffened. After the first glance, Jocelyn walked away and went into his cabin.

CHAPTER 16

It had been a long and tiring voyage and they all showed the strain. The old *Hound of Heaven* was incapacitated in part by the accumulated breakdowns of a trip which had taken a year and which had not touched any place where adequate supplies or fuel could be had.

From Johnny's Landing to Paradise Alcor, from Paradise Alcor to Sweeney Merak, from Sweeney Merak to Coppaccine Dubhe and Coppaccine Dubhe to Earth, or as the pilot had it, to Earth Sun. It was a route known on the long passage as the Big Bear Circuit, touching as it did the main colonies of the constellation Ursus Major alias the Dipper. And things had not been well on Coppaccine Dubhe where on previous trips there had been spare parts. And so it was with something like relief that they entered the outer atmosphere and let Swifty go.

They waited for him with optimism, the women talking of what they would buy, the crewmen happy at the prospect of better food and guns and replacements to ease the strain of watches. But that changed when Swifty came back and the rumor fled through the ship: Earth had been at war. But the war was done and had been done for several hundred years.

Jocelyn drifted down toward their old spaceport and onetime New Chicago. And from the ports, black so long with space dark, a haunted crew looked down on grassy mounds where cattle grazed and at a plain where a drowsy river ran.

And Jocelyn looked at the scribbled scrawl of Swifty's report, squared his shoulders and began to con. They came in two hours above an area which Alan had once known as Colorado and where now stood a sprawling, irregular city some hundreds of miles in extent.

The tired crew and the battered ship eased down, for a spaceport lay below. It was a strange sort of port, but it had a spaceship on it, like a shaft of alabaster. And Jocelyn jockeyed the *Hound of Heaven* down beside it. A rough landing, on the last ounce of her takeoff fuel.

The space locks clanged open and sunlight and air

rushed in. The crew stood by, ready for word from the bridge to "hit dirt." But the word did not come.

Jocelyn looked at the gates of the port and saw that they were metal-gated. He swept a glass around the area from the vantage height of the bridge. It was all enclosed.

And there was not a single human being in sight.

Jocelyn coughed. He looked tired. Since his exposure on a planet, deceptively inviting but poisonous with beryllium oxide, he had not been well. And the rumor had crept quietly through the ship that Strange had said he might die, victim of a loose valve in a space helmet. He pressed a silken handkerchief to his lips, coughed again and turned to Hale.

"What do you make of it?"

"Maybe the whistle just blew," said Hale.

"Corday," said Jocelyn, "step over to that other ship and find out what they know about this place."

Alan saluted and fled down the ladders to the ground air locks. He stepped out into the sunlight, started to take a deep breath and then was struck with a curious foreboding which wiped away all his exultation of being on Earth again. It was so still.

He rapidly covered the distance to the other ship,

reading off her name before he swung up her gangway. She was the *First Fairaway* of Mars.

"Hello, the officer!" he hailed formally.

His voice made a curious echo in the vessel and something made him clutch his sidearm as he stepped through the port.

But she was empty.

He stepped further in, alert. But she was not only empty of men, she was empty of equipment as well. He glanced upwards and found himself looking five hundred feet to her bow ports down which came two eerie shafts of sunlight to dimly light the interior of this hulk. She was without men, without equipment, without decks. Just a hulk.

Alan sped back to the *Hound* and reported tersely.

"Hale," said Jocelyn, "take fifteen men and test the gates. If they are locked, make no overt move but call any human you may see and demand freedom of the port."

Hale grinned. He pulled down a battle helmet, huge as a caldron, buckled a brace of sidearms around his ample middle, stuck a cigar in his face and lighted it. Alan was struck by Hale's exaggerated casualness, by the strangeness of his smile.

"So long, Skipper," said Hale. "Keep your pointers up, Corday." And he dropped down the ladder and was gone.

After a little while they saw him muster his volunteers and fan them out. And then Hale marched across the wide plain of the port to the main gates, his people spread far on each side of him, his weapons in hand.

The party grew small in the distance. The fan contracted a trifle as it neared the main portals. Jocelyn stifled a cough and gave a warning to the bridge deck gunner to look sharp.

But there was no chance of the gunner coming to bear.

With a suddenness which meant long planning and great practice, with a blaze which meant enormous ability in explosives, the ground tore asunder under the party's very feet. And through the gates came long tongues of brilliant orange.

The smoke was heavy but out ahead of it burst Hale, waving his arm to his men to come on. Three struggled up and sought to follow that roaring war cry. And then the gates flamed again, struck out and struck down. Hale stopped. He turned around, staggering, torn almost in half. He fixed his eyes on the ship and half lifted his huge arm. And then once more the gates blazed forth and Hale fell heavily to earth, the last of his party to die.

Alan turned, on the verge of raging fury, ready to kill the bridge gunner where he sat. But reason tugged him and he knew that Hale's closeness to those gates would not admit such a thorough blast as the bridge guns would have made.

The icily emotionless voice of Jocelyn sawed through the stillness of the place. "Turner, load smoke. Fire smoke. Snoozer, pass the word. Smoke."

And the bridge gun snarled as it hurled out charge after charge, bucking and reeling with recoil, and elsewhere in the ship other guns roared into a thundering chorus.

And then they stopped.

An area of ten square miles was blanketed thick with drifting but impenetrable smoke.

"Fire on image!" snapped Jocelyn.

The bridge gunner flicked the switch on his memory plate and began to chop bursts at the gate, now everywhere invisible except in his sights.

"Saturate with G19," said Jocelyn. And Snoozer

spoke into the ship circuits. "Seal the ship!" said Jocelyn.

A moment later the multiple batteries made the hull shake as they hurled charges out into the smoke which, at least in other days, had foiled detectors which might search for the *Hound*.

"Saturate with RG," said Jocelyn.

"Saturate with RG!" said Snoozer.

And the batteries on other decks vibrated as they hurled forth regurgitant gas to cling to the particles of smoke.

She had been used as a merchant vessel. They might have better ashore. She was old and tired and her technology had been theirs uncounted centuries ago. But she fired and sought to defend herself. And the Deuce stared with anger at the empty tubes where there was no takeoff fuel.

Alan had already taken down his helmet and was looking to his gun.

"Battle party stand by the starboard ground lock in full space kit," said Jocelyn.

"Battle party stand by the starboard ground lock in full space kit," repeated Snoozer.

Alan turned alertly to Jocelyn. There had been other battles in the outposts in the stars. And the command of the second battle party would devolve on the remaining mate.

"Where do you think you are going, Mr. Corday?" said Jocelyn, taking his own suit from the hands of Mistress Luck. His spacesuit rustled as he put it on. He fixed the helmet in place, tapped at the voice multiplying switch at his collar to null it for a moment.

Alan sagged as he recognized in this the contempt Jocelyn had always shown him.

"Mr. Corday, I leave you in charge of the vessel. Regardless of what happens to me, you will not quit the ship with her remaining crew but will do all in your power to defend her at her own ports. You are sufficiently informed of these things to sell her not inexpensively should I fail." He took to coughing and the eyes of Mistress Luck were round with concern. He cleared his throat then and continued. "You are young and impulsive and have many faults to overcome. Let no quixotic stupidity lead you to risk this vessel and the women, children and crew which remain within her unless you have clear and unavoidable cause. I will be back, I am sure. Remember that," he added harshly.

Pegging his helmet again, Alan turned away. Behind

him he heard Mistress Luck adjusting buckles on Jocelyn's spacesuit. It was a bitter thing to be so shunted aside. An empty thing, "in charge," for in the absence of all seniors, he had been "in charge" many times before. A tradition. No more. He was obviously not considered trustworthy enough for this task. And yet, twice since Johnny's Landing he had proved himself and proved himself well in the field.

There was a rumble somewhere below as landing force equipment was rolled out. Ancient equipment but it worked and it might serve. Alan knew what Jocelyn would do—blast through an unexpected point, take the besiegers in the rear, detach a small party to scoop up important officials or officers in a swoop raid while all the fireworks and purpose seemed to be directed elsewhere; and they would hold the hostages against supplies. Long-passage practice, timeworn and usually successful.

"Sir," said Irma, the bridge talker on the landing evolution, "can I run down for a minute and tell Joe goodbye?"

"Stand by your post!" said Alan. And he hurled his sidearm back into its holster.

A moment later he was sorry. There would be

people killed in that landing party. And he almost relented but stopped in the act of turning and walked forward to the bridge gun which was unmanned. The memory plate still gleamed with the image of the gate but the gate was certainly no longer there. He faced the detectors. The operator was gone, member of the first landing party, dead now. His replacement had left with Jocelyn. But Alan had installed these things new, last trip in.

He polarized the beams until they righted a path through the swirling density of smoke which now completely obscured the ports, even coated them. Then he sought to tune to get an image. But the protective barrage was too good. There was not even a faint blur on the screens.

Nervously he went over to the communicator ledge. It was ringed with the marks of Swifty's countless bottles and he recalled Swifty.

"Pass the word for Swifty," he told Snoozer. "I want him to count noses still aboard."

Snoozer slid away down a ladder.

Alan was listening intently for any firing outside. It would be hard to hear through this sealed and insulated shell, but it would not be impossible. But he heard no firing. The smoke and its components had gulped up the second landing party and every sight and sound.

Swifty gangled up the ladder. "Got it, Corday. We're trimmed down to five old men, forty engineers and technicians, sixty-eight women, thirty-one kids and thee and me. But I think some of the kids are a bit too young to man a gun. Little chappie back there said, 'Glug, glug,' when I wanted to know his proper emergency station. Had a mouthful of milk."

"Break open the storage arsenals and serve out weapons," said Alan. "Pass the word, all hands in masks and full battle kit, gamma-proof spacesuits. That means *all hands*. That smoke is deadly."

"That isn't all that may get deadly around here, eh? Well, get me a short drink and hobble on my way. But they'll make short work of us, you know, when they begin to feel for us with high-powered stuff."

"The smoke is heated and their detectors won't locate us unless they've got telepathy machines!" snapped Alan. "And they want this ship for what they can salvage out of her. The other was gutted. They won't shoot this way! Don't spread any sad conversation about it."

Swifty shrugged, poured himself a small shot, downed it and gangled below.

Nervously Alan tuned his ears for the sound of firing. There had not been any yet, so far as he could tell. He felt left out of it. The safest post in the whole fight was here. Jocelyn hadn't trusted him enough. But the emergency was great and they were lost entirely if the second landing force failed.

There had been very little wind; the screen would take a long time to dissipate. But he wondered if he might not be wise to create a diversion by banging away into the town at long range. But no, that would bring the attackers here into the desperate necessity of destroying the ship. He would wait it out.

"Post a man outside," he said to the returned Swifty. "I want him to use his ears. Maybe we can tell. Give him a phone."

"Won't that spot us, old boy?"

"That happens to be the least of our worries," said Alan. "Post the man."

"If you say so," shrugged Swifty and gangled off on the errand.

Alan worriedly twisted at his scarf, realized what he was doing and hurriedly stopped. Waiting was hard.

CHAPTER 17

To allay his increasing nervousness Alan concentrated his mind on the possibility of takeoff. But there was no answer there. A ship which used particle drive had to use nonradiant fuel for maneuvering close to ground. And while they had enough high drive to take them back to the stars—having wisely provided against that sometime day when Earth would no longer be able to furnish fuels from herself and sister planets—their alpha supply was done. Even their last landing had almost knocked them apart from conserving the last dyne. To take off on high was unthinkable. Touching off their main power this close to Earth would, with zero initial velocity, simply blow them to pieces, to say nothing of cutting the earth's crust to a depth of forty miles or more and drowning the tiny fragments of ship and man in lava.

He now and then called for a report from his lookout.

Firing had crackled sporadically toward the town for some minutes now but it was impossible to judge what might be happening, beyond the certain knowledge that Jocelyn had made hot contact with something.

It made Alan fume to be standing here, idle, trapped, and to think of his fellow shipmen out there waging war with high odds. If Jocelyn lost—

The ship knew much of what would happen and might be able to guess the rest. If this city merely took the survivors prisoner, the people of the *Hound* were still lost, for their ship would be lost and they, all of them, were millenniums out of phase.

At last Alan sent a messenger groping out toward the firing. The boy did not go far before he returned along the string he had laid, leading a wounded member of Jocelyn's party.

The man was dreadfully ill, his spacesuit opened by some scorching missile, his right arm burned nearly off, his lungs full of RG and smoke. Alan came down the ladders with a rush to the sick bay where they had taken him. It was the detector technician.

Strange and his assistant were stopping the arterial bleeding when Alan came in.

"Get a motor on him and pump out his lungs!" said Alan. "I've got to talk to him."

"Pretty terrible shape," said Strange. "Better let me give him some nerve drain."

"No," said Alan. "He's got to talk. The data he has is more important."

"It might kill him."

"Not knowing might kill this ship!" said Alan. "Do what I tell you!"

Strange sighed and pulled out the tubes of the device they used when suits leaked on planets with poisonous air. He attached it and in a short while, beginning to writhe under the stimulus of an awakening shot, the technician was ready to talk.

Under Alan's insistent hammering he finally answered: "Lost . . . the party into . . . town. I . . . was one of them. Skipper pinned down . . . thousand men . . . no uniforms . . . got funny weapons—"

"Put him to sleep," said Alan.

He pounded a fist into his palm again and again as he went up the ladders, scowling and racked. Suddenly he turned and went back, bypassing the sick bay and diving into the engineering compartment.

The Deuce was there, ears strained to the distant firing, heard faintly through the hull.

"Get your tools. All the men you've got, full kit and follow me!"

"What's up?" said the Deuce.

"Jocelyn is held up, probably superior weapons against him. We've got to work fast."

"Reinforcements?" said the Deuce.

"Follow me!" said Alan.

Snoozer was just behind him. He had not noticed before how close she had stuck. "Pass the word, all hands full space kit, outside."

She darted off and in a short time Alan stood beside the after-lock watching the ghostly shapes of the crew assembling in the swirls of smoke outside. There were not many left. Most of them women, some of them carrying babies, all of them carrying weapons.

"Thought we were to stay—" began Swifty.

"Deuce," said Alan. "Take your people aft. Call anyone else you'll need for work or transport. Dismount a high drive and its load."

"Do what?" said Deuce, a thin shadow in the smoke.

"Do as you're told," said Alan.

Deuce, puzzled, called off several names and vanished. Alan withdrew the rest from the vicinity of the ship after checking that none were now aboard but two sick and the assistant to care for them.

Alan posted Bill the Eye with a pack communicator near the ship and gave the equipment mate of it to Irma, already burdened with a two-year-old.

"You stand by," said Alan to Bill. "Jocelyn or any survivors come back, route them compass north and up the east side of the hill above here. You saw it coming in? The town lies mainly west. Bad terrain east of it. Tell anyone to come up the east slope to the crest and under no circumstances to approach the hill from the west or they may get shot."

"Sure," said Bill.

Alan fumbled through the smoke to the engineers working on the drive and gave them the benefit of his shoulder. They had it dismounted in seven minutes, long practiced from changing drives in full flight. And they wrapped ropes around it so that it could be carried.

With a final check on Bill, Alan led off by compass. Half his party were engaged with the drive's transport, the remainder were spread out as flankers and rearguard. Alan and two engineers with disintegrating torches led the van.

"How yer know we can climb that hill?" panted the Deuce behind Alan. "And how do yer know if it's even there?"

"Anyone trained in surveying notices topography," said Alan. "And compass directions. Pass the word now to be as quiet as possible and keep close."

When they reached the metal fence to the north, almost colliding with it in the dense smoke, Alan let go with the torches and burned out a hundred-foot section. He threw a scouting party through this and then called up his main body.

They passed through a dimly seen residential area and trod twice on unmasked men in agonies of vomiting in the street, a sight which greatly cheered them all.

Pressing on through the smoke they came to rising ground. It was steep and here everyone had to lend a hand on the ropes. The drive, usually handled by cranes or in the ungravity of cruising, did not offer an easy problem in this precipitous ascent.

So engrossed were they and so heavy was the

smoke that they came solidly into a blockhouse, point-blank. Swifty, in the van, fired fast and heaved a grenade in at the door. Unmolested they went on up.

Blowing and wheezing they came at length to the hogback of the ridge and began to ease the drive down.

"If I knew what you were doing—" complained the Deuce.

"Bear a hand," said Alan.

Two hundred feet down they came to a hillside home, built here as some rich man's whim, clinging to the perpendicular but commanding a view. A track went down from it, a private railway.

Two servants were present, clawing in exhausted misery at the boards of the sun porch. Alan crisply ordered a spare mask to be put on the man. He gave no second thought to the woman.

Thrusting pack spades deep into the formal garden they butted in the drive, angling up its nose until Alan was satisfied. People not intimate with the engineering department were happy to get away from it, suspicious of its radioactiveness and none too confident of the ability of their spacesuits to prevent burns, and none too confident of Strange's serum against gamma rays with which they all were customarily shot when it was put this near to a test.

With the others retired, Alan and the Deuce installed a throttle and an igniter and the engine was ready to do its customary duty in an unaccustomed setting.

Alan went into the house and attempted to question the manservant, but the fellow was too terrified to talk and when shot with a catalyst was too exhausted to do anything more than sleep. Disgusted at the balk of his needs, Alan ranged the place, looking for the phone. He passed it several times without seeing what it was, for he had supposed that the wall screen was video. Then he found what he wanted, an index book of the city. The town, he found, squinting through face-plate and smoke at the strange script, seemed to be known as St. Denniston and the main exchange was Denver. Then he sighed with relief and gave himself a little more air to clear his thoughts and perceptions.

In the back of the book was a map of exchanges for the purpose of long distance and after that was another map of the central section. It was difficult to read the printing, but by checking against the index itself he found what he wanted to know. They had landed at the capital city of the "Third Estate" and from the frequency in the book of the name "Consoundalin" he concluded that it was the individual in power. He cross-checked what he had found with a basket full of tape which proved to be a newspaper and discovered he was right. He tore a page from the book and went back to the drive.

There was a little more shifting and then Alan sent all of his party up the hill and over the crest. Keeping the Deuce and Snoozer with him he unreeled throttle wire down the slope and to the right until they found another residence, a quarter of a mile from the first.

Here were other servants, all ill, all too deep in their own exhaustion to be interested. No "upper class" was in the house but there was a big wall screen there. The Deuce fumbled with it for a while and at length discovered that by sitting down on the seat beside it, it lighted.

A girl glowed into three-dimensional being on the screen, a pretty girl, white, without much on.

"Give me Command 1," said Alan.

She frowned, trying to understand what he meant, and then asked for a repeat.

"Huh!" said the Deuce. "If that's the language now, I'm glad I'm on the long passage!"

Alan held up the torn index, pointing to the number. The screen blurred, showed a pretty picture during the wait and then flashed on as an office. Both the exchange and this office were obviously beyond any smoke pall the old *Hound* could hope to throw. There was a grand unconcern on the military aide's debonair face when he looked up and spoke.

"This is the *Hound of Heaven*," said Alan. "Sec—First Mate Corday speaking."

"Eh?" said the aide after the fashion of aides speaking to inferiors. "Eh?"

Alan was talking lingua spacia and the aide finally grasped the fact, grasped it with some surprise. He stood up and called to another office and a man in a naval uniform entered, the naval aide.

"This is the *Hound of Heaven*," said Alan.

"Really?" said the naval aide. "And what would that be?"

"A ship from the long passage," said Alan.

The aide tensed and then relaxed with a smile. "Didn't know you had a phone, you know. Interesting hook-in, isn't it? Understand you're in a trifle of a jam.

Might tell me what your cargo is. The old man is interested in cargoes since the embargo."

"I don't think you'll particularly care about our cargo," said Alan. "The way you are trying to buy it, it will come too high."

"You mean the fellows at the port," said the aide. "I suppose you've been gone two or three years and won't realize that it's criminal to land. Forfeit all your cargo to land. You're calling to surrender, of course."

"I'm calling to give you five minutes to call off your pups," said Alan.

"Oh?"

"For if you don't, you aren't going to have a town."

"Oh, really?" said the naval aide with the smile aides manage in talking to inferiors.

"I hesitate to give you proof," said Alan. "It will cost you several thousand citizens."

"I assure you," said the naval aide, "that the relief of such a number of populace would be a godsend."

"Even if it includes yourself?"

"What a bluff. Well, I respect you for it. Now if you want to surrender, we'll give you safe conduct out of the spaceport—"

"If you don't surrender this town to me in two minutes,

you're going to get a full load, straight from our bows!"

"Really—"

"Really! I withdraw the two minutes. I'll fire one burst and be back. In ten bursts there'll be no St. Denniston."

"Deeniston," said the naval aide. "I—"

Alan pulled the Deuce off the switch. They unreeled the line into the basement, braced themselves against the wall nearest the drive a quarter of a mile away and closed the switch.

The ground rumbled.

Alan opened the switch.

They waited for a few seconds and then, checking their suits, went back to the first floor. One wall of the house was blown in but the phone worked.

"Command 1," said Alan, pointing to the torn index page.

The girl was shaking, sticking to her post but glancing back of her, unable to concentrate fully.

"Command 1—"

No pretty picture this time. The girl put in her plug and collapsed across the board.

The naval aide was still there but the office had changed. Pictures had fallen from the walls and there was a fog of dust which, combined with the smoke in the room where Alan stood, made the image wavy.

Before the naval aide could speak, a towering man rushed in, falling over the skirts of a golden robe. He was shouting unintelligible things.

"If that is Consoundalin," said Alan in lingua spacia, "tell him he's a hostage." He held up the switch, close to the screen so that the aide could see it, so that Consoundalin could see it. "When I press this again, another blast begins. I don't know what you know of this but it's high drive. Another blast to another quarter of town will double your casualties. Do you surrender?"

There was a gibbering conference interrupted by cross phone connections which screamed about damage.

"I guarantee your health," said Alan. "You and your boss, mister. But if you don't deliver yourselves at the gates of the port in five minutes and if you don't call off all hostilities this instant, another blast starts."

Consoundalin pushed a purpling face at his screen when he heard this translated. Then, suddenly, he sagged and reached for a switch to connect him with his looting parties.

Alan left the Deuce with switch in hand, sent Snoozer to recall his party and, with a sporting weapon he had snatched from the walls of the home, raced down the slope for the spaceport.

CHAPTER 18

The smoke was clearing down. There was no firing. But through the thinning haze the *Hound* could be seen. And there were strange soldiers about her and a hole in her midships where artillery had ranged her.

Alan cared little for that. He was looking wildly along the buildings to find any remnant of the ship party. Then in a street outside the port he saw piles of uniformed bodies, nearly a regiment, and saw that they faced a thick-walled building which had been used as an operations office when the port was active.

He saw a group of men lying on their arms, also facing the building, and knew that at least some were left alive inside. Knowing this he ran back to the gate and arrived there as a huge globular shape skidded to a halt. Out of it climbed the naval aide, three other gentlemen and Consoundalin. Alan wasted no time.

Suddenly hot with anger, he gestured that the

vehicle be sent away, and it went. Then he indicated that he wanted all troops withdrawn from the area and in a short time the naval aide came back to report that they had gone. Alan saw them marching up a street and he turned, white-lipped and shaking to Consoundalin.

"I don't know how you came to power or what devil's society you govern, but you are a disgrace to mankind. Don't bother translating that," said Alan to the aide. "Order them to disrobe."

There was protest at this but not for long. These men had just driven through streets clogged with dead, had plowed their way through panicked mobs, had passed over the ruin of buildings with their dying still inside.

Alan waved them to a wall. "You are my hostages. If I get everything I require here, you will be restored and go free. If I do not, you will die. That is simple. Carrying it out will be simpler yet."

Consoundalin snarled something and the naval aide said, "He says you're a demon. A moment before you called we had the ship in there under attack. It is not fair. You were not firing from your ship! The switchboard girl died and we had no way to trace where you were. What brimstone work is this?"

"Something hotter than brimstone!" said Alan. He found himself aching to kill these men for the damage they had done, for the people they had shot down— and all for the loot of a cargo. Swifty came.

"Guard these people. Take them into the ship and put irons on them and post them before a lower port where, night and day, they will be visible to the curious who want to know if they are still alive. I think this king or whatever here has instilled terror enough in them that they will fear to attack in case he goes free unscathed, for then his vengeance would hit them." He turned to Bill the Eye, scratched and bruised in resisting the ship attackers. "You heard those orders. Pass the word. These men are to remain alive as our only hope."

He was free then and he turned a contemptuous back on his prisoners and hastened to the operations office.

He hailed it from a distance. Its walls, resistant to takeoff blasts, remained silent. He came nearer, keeping in plain sight, walking over the mounded dead, kicking aside strange, powerful weapons.

It was silent in the building, a silence heightened by the moaning wounded in the street. Alan thumped the door with his pistol butt and it echoed hollowly within.

He waited, feeling the oppression of the place as though he stood before a tomb. He tried the lock and then stood back to look at the structure. He walked quickly around it and to the back. There was a blank wall here except for a single door. It was ajar and Alan pushed at it.

The place was carnage.

The dead were racked along the wall, each one at a post. The wounded had dragged themselves to the center of the room to die. And before a window slit, through which still pointed his outmoded blaster, lay Captain Jocelyn, his face serene in death.

Alan took another lagging step into the dimness and then saw what obscured the bloodstained white of Jocelyn's clothes. It was another who should never have been there, who had come there well after the last of the fight.

Mistress Luck lay dead across her captain's body, her small sharp knife plunged deep into her heart.

CHAPTER 19

The ship rumbled with the energy of laboring men, townsmen and crewmen. The high, shrill crackle of torches blended with the thud of hammers and the complaint of heavily laden drills. A rack had been improvised under the Deuce's direction, ancient storehouses and plants had been ransacked for spares and replacements. But little besides weapons was new in this society.

He had not gone near Jocelyn's cabin. They had buried their captain that morning on a knoll, his mistress and his dead beside him, where the stars could look down. And the heavy sadness which had pervaded the crew was jarred with the ferocity of this work.

There had been no question about Alan, no contest of any kind. Since the moment they had known, every remaining man, woman and child in the crew had given him every courtesy, first because of their soared respect for him, second because none could compare with him. And so he went now, heavily, into the cabins where once an admiral had commanded in some far-off and forgotten day.

He was a little amazed to see a letter on the desk addressed to him. It was notched into the corner of a blotter and on it was scrawled "Mr. Corday, in event of my death."

A chilly thing. It had been written weeks and weeks before this recent action according to its ship date. It had been written while Jocelyn still snarled at him and gave him contempt.

He stood where he had often stood under the captain's wrath and he opened it and read:

HOUND OF HEAVEN
Ship-Year 55—1025th watch.

Alan Corday
Sometime Noble and Surveyor-engineer of sometime
New Chicago.

My dear Alan:

I will not say a great deal about the conditions under which you read this. They are very much in the hands of God, who grows, according to Dr. Strange, nearer to me than

I would care to have. Suffice that you have now buried me and come here to look at my effects. They are yours, such as they are, a strange hotchpotch of vanity and memory, all that remains of Duard Henry Jocelyn, sometime captain of the Solar Guards.

Alan, I have much which pleads your forgiveness, beyond the much I have elsewhere had to do. The day you came to me in that saloon, I tricked you. I had to. And even as I spoke to Hale my hand signal said to him to take you at whatever cost. For in these many years of ranging I had not seen my successor. I picked you then.

And I broke you into an officer, Alan, with means you will despise. I ask your pardon now. A long while back, I ordered Queen to propose a mutiny. That gave you will to learn and profit by your thirst for my blood. And I commanded Strange to make you ill so that your watch count would be lost. And I built your hope for early return to Earth and kept you learning and watching how to make us come back. And then, God forgive me now, I broke your heart.

I know not what you felt, Alan, when you went into your town with the hope of ten years gone. But I can estimate your feelings. You see, Alan, it was that way I began upon the long, long passage. And my sweetheart was dead, dead a dozen years before I came back. So I have some inkling, had some even when I did that terrible thing to you.

And you came back to the ship. Two men were never out of your vicinity while you were ashore. For you had long since been appointed in my place by me. And you learned. And I gave you contempt.

You had been withheld from the particular friendship of one or another in the crew. I caused it. Command can have no friends. As you have come to this moment, beside my desk, a lonely man and in command.

Hale could not succeed me. Many things he does not know. Show him the accompanying note of authority and he will obey you. Show this to the crew and they, too, are at your command. But I have no idea that you will need it. They think much more of you than you suspect, Alan. It was my policy to make you believe they did not.

And now you have command. And what you will do with it is your concern. But permit me to tell you an answer to a question you have asked, asked many times, Alan. You want to know why?

You have been in many actions on many strange planets. You have seen strange things. And you have watched our Earth ebb and flow.

Earth will not live forever. And, unless he is helped, neither will man.

We could land on some fertile planet and take our ease, put aside the risks of travel, make ourselves comfortable and at *home*. But this ship must be our home and this task must be ours as it is the task of many another ship on the long passage.

You have seen sentient races living on our technologies or inventing their own. Do you want them to outlast our breed? Do you want those other species to inherit at last our Universe? I think not, Alan. I think you will go on.

This is the crusade of the long passage, a lonely and unthanked crusade.

Man shall triumph at last amongst the stars.

Man, not Achnoids, not Gleenites, not crawling things, can and must survive.

This ship and her sisters in the stars and on the

passage are, without the slightest help from Earth, the *only* means which shall cause man to survive as a race and triumph everywhere.

Do not curse equations. Someday man will conquer Time. Until he does, Alan, you and men like you, and ships like the *Hound*, will bless those equations which let us go at all, land with such swiftness, carry on the race, the triumphs, the hope of man.

I wish you luck in your command and luck amongst the stars, the loyalty of our crew and the friendship of our colonies which we so strangely serve. And perhaps someday, if the priests are right, I can shake your hand, Alan, and hear from you the job you did.

God bless you.

Good luck.

I trust you. And all I had and hoped for, all are yours.

Jocelyn

Alan put it gently down and for a long while stood oblivious of the ship, his mind ranged back across the bridge of years. And then he turned and quickly walked out upon the bridge. His sight was queerly misted and it took him a little time to see the repairs in progress there.

Then he began to inspect them and gradually to put to rights the ship and the day.

In the afternoon there came a number of learned gentlemen and he gave them coldness. A reporter was with them and took down many notes so that he could publish the advantages of treating well the long-passage ships.

And Alan grew cunning and told them that in the stars and amongst the colonies there were many weapons and that long-passage ships, coming home even after the lapse of centuries, still could lay low this society. And he told them of a means of communication in the long passage which did not exist and said he had already sent the word to other ships to be wary. And, who knew? It might help the next.

And he went into town at dusk and looked at it and found books published after their last time on Earth. He went to a stew and he spread talk there about riches and the fabulous spaceman's life which was all gain and no work whatever. And he stood aloof while his crew inveigled men and women into signing through the night and he shipped, on the morrow, with his newspaper story out, five hundred colonists and all necessary equipment, shipped them for an "uncultivated island on Venus where food springs up from the ground overnight."

And all that day and the next he haggled for stores and books and goods, holding aloof, paying for what he got in the cargo they had brought, making it most interestingly wealthy for merchants to deal with the long-passage ship and insinuating that trade was no monopoly of their monarch but the right of free-born citizens of the merchant class.

And then the ship was loaded, all repairs were made, and they were done.

CHAPTER 20

Alan stood on the bridge. A military officer was bowing his way out. "You will land them from the lifeboat, then, Captain Corday."

Coldly, Alan looked at him. The man was oily. No wonder he had come so high in a debauched court. No wonder he could exist in a society where, as Alan had seen on the day before, human meat hung in shops for sale.

"I generally keep my word," said Alan. "It would not pay just now to break it. They will be landed as and when I have said."

"Thank you, oh, thank you, Captain Corday." And the man was gone.

A young engineer of the port had come into the bridge to give the instruments a last check. Alan had seen him before, a well-educated alert young man who knew his job. Alan watched him. He was thinking of old

Hale and the rest on the ridge up there, a ridge bathed in sunlight today.

There was a quiver of expectancy in the ship. The word had been passed. People were coming to their stations for takeoff—short-handed just now with the new crewmen so untrained. What would those crewmen think, some of them, who did not know about the long passage and its Time?

The engineer finished with the new detecting equipment and turned to make an adjustment on the drive communicator.

Swifty came up on the bridge to take station. He had a bottle in his hand and he put it down on the customary ledge. He was only slightly drunk. Other crewmen were here on station already, alertly watching their captain.

"Mr. Roston," said Alan coolly. Swifty looked up in surprise. It had been years since he had heard his real name.

"Mr. Roston," said Alan, "I have today shipped a new atmosphere pilot and taken into the lock a new plane."

Swifty had not known this. He stared, startled, uncertain.

"A long time ago," said Alan, "you were in a war. You

were very young. You have grown older. I think it is time you forgot that war, Mr. Roston." He walked to the ledge and picked up the new bottle. He turned and threw it butt first against the bulkhead. The loud crash of it froze the bridge.

"Take your post, Mr. Roston," said Alan. "From this moment forward you are first mate of this vessel. You know your duties. Perform them. Is that clear?"

The young engineer from the port was staring at the shattered glass which had so barely missed a communicator panel. He had finished with his adjustment and now he saw how near was the ship to leaving and approached the ladder.

"A moment there," said Alan. The engineer turned. "Do you know of the long passage?"

"Good lord, sir," said the engineer, "I have a good job where I am."

"The long passage pays better," said Alan.

"And has a great deal wrong with its time equations," said the engineer. "Only a madman would attempt such a thing as a volunteer. Thank you for the offer but I have responsibilities here."

Alan looked at him appraisingly. He motioned with his hand to the quartermaster. "Take that man into custody and hold him in sick bay until we have cleared Earth."

The engineer's face hardened as he looked into the pale, tired features of Alan Corday. He rushed and the spacemen present sought to block him. But he got through.

Alan brought his pistol butt down smartly on the engineer's skull. He dropped, breathing hard, still half-conscious. He struggled half up.

"But you can't . . . you can't . . . my wife—"

They took him below.

"All stations report ready," said Alan. And waited.

"Ready, sir," said Irma.

"You will take off and set a course for Johnny's Landing, Mr. Roston. You will set the proper watches and find a proper relief for yourself amongst our original crew. Understood?"

Mr. Roston drew himself up smartly, a piece of shattered bottle ground under his heel. "Aye, aye, Captain." He faced about and began to snap the necessary orders.

The low drives trembled. The ship began to lift. The prisoners went into the lifeboat and, at ninety miles altitude, were shoved away.

Alan walked slowly into his cabin. His own pitiful collection of gear was there in the otherwise empty drawers and lockers. He sat down in the chair before the desk, looking at nothing.

A phrase was ringing in his ears: "You can't . . . my wife—" And he saw again a night when it had rained and heard again a weirdly beautiful concerto played on a piano in a stew.

His head ached brutally and his nerves were taut. He looked at the desk. A bottle of brandy was there and a sheaf of small packets, just as Jocelyn had left them. Corday poured a drink and then, with a sudden, savage motion, emptied into it the contents of a paper. He drank it down.

Behind them a city had dropped from sight, a city overlooked by a knoll, a city which had paid a terrible price for treachery.

The drink and drug began to take effect. Alan felt somebody near him and he turned. Snoozer stood at the door, face calm, waiting. She wore a pleasant dress and a new bracelet on her arm. She was no longer fourteen. She was a woman grown, a lovely woman as Alan suddenly saw. He looked at her and wondered that he had not seen before.

The Countess entered the room and closed the door.

And high into the black, black void the *Hound of Heaven* sped, upward bound and outward bound on a mission to the ageless stars.

GLOSSARY

ACEY-TRAYS: (also acey-treys) A card game; apparently a variant of acey-deucy poker.

AIR WEEBLES: A space illness.

ALPHA CENTAURI: A first magnitude star, 4.3 light-years from the Sun, also called Rigel (or Rigil) Kentaurus, the star closest to the Sun.

ALPHA SUPPLY: Referring to the amount of remaining alpha fuel, the fuel used for takeoff. An alpha particle is a positively charged particle given off by certain radioactive substances.

APPETITE OVER TIN CUP: A pioneer Western United States term used by riverboat men on the Missouri, meaning thrown away violently like "head over heels," "bowled over."

BLOUSE: The upper outer garment of any uniform.

BLOWSY: Coarse, untidy and red-faced; said of a woman.

BONE UP: (slang) To study intensely, cram.

BRIC-A-BRAC: Superfluous or inconsequential items or matters.

BRIMSTONE: Sulfur. According to the Bible, the fires of Hell were pits of burning brimstone.

CABIN: From *cabin class*, the class of accommodations on a passenger ship less costly and less luxurious than first class, but more so than tourist class.

CAPTAIN'S RUNNER: The captain's messenger.

CELESTOLABE: A device for celestial navigation.

CHEROOT: A cigar cut off square at both ends.

COHORT: A company, band or group.

CON/CONNED: (nautical) The station or post of the person who steers a vessel or the act or process of steering a vessel.

CONSTANT (OR c): Referring to the speed of light, 186,000 miles per second.

COQUETRY: Effort or action intended to attract others; flirtation.

CUD: The regurgitated contents of certain animals' stomachs, which they rechew after eating.

CURVED-SPACE COMPUTATION: An interstellar navigational procedure that factors in the curvature of space.

DESCRIPTIVE GEOMETRY: A branch of geometry that solves three-dimensional problems.

Driveman: One who assists in the running of the drives aboard the ship.

Dyne: A unit of force most commonly used in theoretic physics. A force is a "push" or "pull" experienced by a mass when it is accelerated.

Eclipsing: A cutting off or extinction of something.

Enfilade: To be in a position to rake with gunfire in a lengthwise action.

Extra-Atmosphere Travel: Travel in outer space, beyond the atmosphere of the planet.

Fatigue Cap: Working uniform cap.

Fission: A nuclear reaction in which a nucleus splits into smaller nuclei with the simultaneous release of energy.

Footpad: A highwayman or robber who goes on foot.

Gs: (slang) Short for grand, a grand or "G" being a thousand dollars.

Gammas: Gamma ray(s), a high-frequency radiation emitted from the nucleus of a radioactive atom.

Gow-eater: One who eats opium; an opium addict.

Gravity Jigs: Space illness.

HCL: (chemistry) Hydrogen chloride; a colorless, corrosive gas of pungent, suffocating odor.

Hooker: (nautical slang) Any old-fashioned or clumsy vessel.

H.T.U.: Halloland Thermal Units. Currently the term **BTU** or *British Thermal Units* is used as a measure of heat. One BTU is a unit of heat equal to about 252 calories, the amount needed to raise the temperature of one pound of water one degree Fahrenheit.

Icebox: Extra-vehicular atmosphere, referring to the cold of deep space.

Instanter: At once.

Jig: A half-ounce measure.

Jigger: A small cup or glass used to measure liquor.

Languid: Lacking energy or interest.

Lardulous: Fat.

Lark: Playful, frivolous adventure or antic; something done just for fun.

Limn: To outline in clear, sharp detail.

Lingua Spacia: The common language of space.

Lotus of Mizar Puronic: A type of fur.

Lurid Press: Publications given to shocking or sensational stories.

Man-o'-war: Warship.

Metonic Locators: Referring to a means of identifying another ship.

Mort: A great quantity or number.

Narcohypnosis: The process of putting a subject under one's control through the administration of drugs followed by hypnotic suggestion and commands.

Nonradiant Fuel: Referring to fuel that does not radiate.

On Dirt: On a planet's surface.

Oncet: (colloquial) Once.

Pariah: One who is shunned or despised by others; outcast.

Particle Drive: Referring to the use of atomic particles to run the engines of the spaceship.

Passage-Beg: The exchange of work for the ticket price of a journey.

Piped the Belly: The pipe is the boatswain's (bosun's) whistle, a silver pipe used by him to convey orders to the crew; in this case, to call the crew to the mess where meals were served.

Pittance: Very small or inadequate sum of money.

Plate Fleet: Fleets of Spanish ships which carried manufactured goods for sale to the citizens of the New World, and were then filled with the rich treasures of the Americas for transport back to Spain.

Plug: A wad of chewing tobacco.

Proof/Proofed: To make one resistant to hypnotic suggestion and hypnosis.

Psi Particle: A type of subatomic particle.

Quixotic: Foolish, impractical, romantic, as the lead character in Miguel de Cervantes' novel *Don Quixote*.

Racks: The structure on which spacecraft land.

Rebuffs: Blunt or abrupt rejections.

RG: Regurgitant Gas; gas which makes one vomit.

Rigel Kentaurus: (also Rigil) Another name for Alpha Centauri.

Ritocrat: An upper class personage, as *aristocrat*.

Salaam: A salutation performed by bowing low and usually clasping the hands together or touching the right hand to the forehead.

Sawbones: A physician or surgeon.

Skidded: Taken advantage of or caused to fail.

Space Artist: From the original nautical term *artist*, a mariner of former days who was versed in navigation when the practice of the science was considered an accomplishment.

Spectrum Navigation: The concept of being able to identify stars and their location and then navigate to them through the use of the spectrum.

Stew: A cheap, disreputable saloon, gambling place or dive.

Swell: A person of a high social position.

Thermalon: A type of fuel.

TIME DIFFERENTIAL: Referring to the concept central to the story that travelers on the long passage had virtually no time elapse during their journey, while Earth time marched ahead at its normal rate.

TRICK: (nautical) A turn of duty at the helm.

VERMINOUS: Resembling or infested with vermin, as insects, lice, etc.

WARDROOM: The messroom assigned to officers on a warship.

WATCH ON WATCH: (nautical) From *watch and watch*; the arrangement in which the two halves or watches of a ship's crew are on duty alternately every four hours at sea. On the **Hound of Heaven**, the watches are changed every five hours.